Praise for *The Blue Note*

"David Keller has gathered a treasure trove of new information and images about Musicians' Union Local 493, the cradle of Seattle's early jazz scene."

- Paul de Barros, *Seattle Times* jazz critic and author of *Jackson Street After Hours: The Roots of Jazz in Seattle*

"Keller knows this subject well and writes keenly of it. The book bubbles over with captivating prose, photographs, and insightful interviews that show a masterful grasp of the issues involved. To the reader's benefit, he occasionally lets his musician subjects expound on their working lives. These are some of the most heartwarming stories in the book."

-Doug Barnett, Co-author of *Historical Dictionary of African American Theatre*

"A magnificent job of research and writing... truly an informative, classy book. The format, with the photos adjacent to the text, provides the reader with immediate visual access to the written material, a highly original and welcome approach."

-Mimi Melnick, former *Los Angeles Times* jazz critic

"David Keller's *The Blue Note* is a unique treasure trove packed with 100 years of fascinating photos and detailed information, to which I frequently return, connecting today's vibrant jazz community with its deep roots."

-Steve Griggs, Associate Producer for the *Impulse! Records* release, "A Love Supreme: Live in Seattle" and contributing writer to *Earshot Jazz* magazine.

"*The Blue Note* takes me home to the heady days of Seattle's jazz scene. It's a fine blend of rare photographs, first person accounts and solid scholarship. It also shines light on the path-breaking union musicians who played Seattle and ultimately brought about the merging of the black and white unions."

-Quincy Jones

This book documents a portion of American cultural history not often chronicled. Focused on Seattle's black American Federation of Musicians' Local 493, it is an upbeat story of race, jazz, gender, and union culture, set in the Pacific Northwest and the wider jazz world. Detailed research and end notes underpin a user-friendly pictorial format, spanning the years from the 1880s to the mid-1950s. *The Blue Note* uses union documents, first person oral histories, and extensive primary and secondary sources. The book features more than 100 photographs and other illustrations, many previously unpublished.

David Keller is an archivist and historian with a strong interest in labor and jazz history. He co-authored *There and Back: The Roy Porter Story* for Louisiana State University Press and has written for various publications, including *Down Beat, Jazz Times, COLUMBIA* and *BlackPast.org*.

The Blue Note
Seattle's Black Musicians' Union
- A Pictorial History -

DAVID KELLER

Copyright © 2024 by David Keller.

Fifth, Revised Edition

This book was generously supported by grants from the 4Culture Special Projects Program. Additional editorial and design help for this revised edition was provided by Linda Bathgate and Kerry Darnall at Washington State University Press, as well as by designer Juan E. G. Doria.

All rights reserved. No part of this publication may be reproduced or transmitted in any form or by any means, electronic or mechanical, including photocopy, recording, or any information storage or retrieval system, without permission in writing from the author.

Every effort has been made to properly credit photographs and text. Errors or omissions brought to the author's attention will be corrected in subsequent editions.

To Shelly Parsons, Megan, Jack, and the enduring magic of music.

Contents

Illustrations vii

Foreword by Brian J. Carter xi

Acknowledgements xiii

Introduction xvii

The Blue Note 1

Appendix 175

Notes 179

Bibliography 193

Index 201

Illustrations

1. Powell Barnett Sr., circa 1895 3
2. Powell Barnett Jr. in Roslyn Band Uniform, c. 1900s 5
3. Roslyn Marching Band, c. 1920 7
4. Cast & Band at the Dixieland, 1909 9
5. Volunteers of America Marching Band, c. 1911 11
6. Whang Doodle Orchestra, 1915-1918 13
7. Jelly Roll Morton, c. 1927 15
8. Gertrude Wright, c. 1920 17
9. Wagner's Band Poem, 1922 19
10. Edythe Turnham Five, c. 1923. 21
11. The Black Hawks, 1926-1928 21
12. Frank Waldron & the Odeon Jazz Orchestra, c. 1925 23
13. Jimmy Adams Collegiate 4, c. 1926 25
14. Mamie Smith & Her Jazz Hounds, c. 1923 27
15. Bessie Smith in St. Louis Blues, c. 1929 29
16. Eddie Peabody, c. 1927 31
17. Paul Whiteman & Charles "Tiny" Burnett, c. 1930 33
18. Herb Wiedoeft & His Boys, 1927 34
19. Egyptian Honeymoon, 1927 35
20. Vic Meyers Orchestra, c. 1928 37
21. Black & Tan Jazz Orchestra, c. 1928 39
22. Luis Russell Big Band, 1931 41
23. 493 AFM Delegate Badge, 1932 43
24. Gene Coy & Rhythm Section, 1938 45
25. That Naughty Waltz, 1920 46
26. The Manila Troubadours, c. 1933 47
27. The Moonlight Serenaders, 1933 49
28. Meet the Duke, 1934 51
29. Champion Drum Beater, 1935 53
30. Highness of Hi-De-Ho, 1935 55
31. Earl Whaley's Orchestra, 1937 57
32. Bar-B-Que at 411, 1938 59
33. Dick Wilson with Andy Kirk, 1941 61
34. The Savoy Boys, c. 1941 63
35. Al Pierre Band, c. 1945 65
36. Dorothy Lomax at the black Elks Club, c. 1942 67
37. Royal Colored Giants, late 1940s 69
38. Carver Athletic Club, 1949 69
39. The 908 Club, mid-1940s 71
40. Seattle's 458 & 493 Union, Hall & Club Locations 73
41. Gerald Wells & Band at Todd's, c. 1943-1944 77

42. Slum Boulevard at Any Street, 1944 79
43. Hustle & Bustle, mid-1940s 81
44. Buddy Catlett, c. 1980s 83
45. Buddy Groves, c. 1940s 85
46. Jive Bombers in Uniform, c. 1940s 87
47. Local 493 Price List, 1949 89
48. William Funderberg Big Band, 1940 91
49. Melody Jones Band & the Kitty, 1945 93
50. Sy Groves & Katherine Dunham, mid-1940s 95
51. Gerald Wiggins, 1986 97
52. Blowing the Blues Away, 1948 99
53. Princess Zenobia Jefferson, c. 1940 101
54. Washington Social & Educational Club Playbill, c. 1946 103
55. Rex Stewart & Jive Bombers, c. 1946 105
56. Bumps Blackwell, c. 1949 107
57. Ella Fitzgerald & the Four Keys, c. 1942 109
58. Fats Waller, 1941 111
59. International Sweethearts of Rhythm, c. 1944 113
60. Russell Jones & Palmer Johnson, 1944 115
61. Louis Armstrong, 1942 117
62. Cab Calloway, 1943 118
63. Duke Ellington, c. 1943 118
64. Lucky Millinder & Noble Sissle, 1943 119
65. Dee Dee Hacket, c. 1944-1945 121
66. Jitterbugging, Seattle, c. 1944 123
67. One Night at the Black & Tan, c. 1946 125
68. Merle Fuller Quartet at the Rizal Club, 1944 127
69. Northwest All-Star Concert, 1946 129
70. Norm Bobrow Presents, 1946 129
71. The Union Club, c. 1947 131
72. The Rocking Chair, mid-1940s 132
73. At Todd's with Satchmo et. al., c. 1945-1946 133
74. At the Spinning Wheel, c. 1946 134
75. Club Lido, mid-1940s 135
76. Tolerance & the Beat, mid-1940s 137
77. Flying Home, 1946 139
78. Jimmy White Trio, c. 1949-1950 141
79. Appearing Nightly, c. 1950 142
80. Travelling Dues, 1948-1951 143
81. The Blue Note, c. 1953 145
82. Local 493 Officers, 1953 146
83. Musicians' Union Cards, 1949-1976 147
84. Ray Charles Robinson & Private Clifford Radney, 1950 149
85. Ernestine Anderson & Ray Charles Robinson, 1950 149
86. First Integrated Dance, 1950 151
87. Patti Bown, c. 1958 153
88. Ebony Café, c. 1956 155

89.	Breakfast Jam, c. 1956	155
90.	At The Blue Note, 1996	157
91.	Ernie Hatfield, 1957	158
92.	At Coe's Tavern, 1957	159
93.	Floyd Standifer, 1983	161
94.	Pete's Poop-Deck, 1962	163
95.	Jabo Ward at Pete's, 1959	163
96.	The Penthouse, 1962	163
97.	Ben & Ed Laigo, 1959	165
98.	Jam Session at The Door, 1959	165
99.	Bud Schultz Trio, 1959	165
100.	Frank Roberts Trio, 1957	167
101.	Frank Roberts Quartet, 1959	167
102.	Quincy Jones Big Band, 1959	169
103.	Tolerance Personified, c. 1949-1950	171
104.	Lifetime Membership, 1951	173
105.	493 Membership List, page 1	175
106.	493 Membership List, page 2	176
107.	493 Membership List, page 3	177

x

Foreword

Brian J. Carter
Executive Director, 4Culture

I first met David Keller in 2009 while working as the Deputy Director/Head Curator at the Northwest African American Museum (NAAM). Having just opened our doors the year prior, I was hard at work pulling together a new show exploring the vivacious jazz spectacle that was Seattle's Jackson Street during the '30s, '40s and '50s. This project would utilize an existing photography exhibition, compiled by journalist and author Paul DeBarros, with the addition of objects and stories from auxiliary jazz scenes in Portland and Spokane.

David came down to the museum for a visit and shared the treasure trove of stories, photographs, and objects he had painstakingly assembled to resurrect the story of Seattle's Black Musicians' Union, Local 493. I remember excitedly discussing the personalities, nightclubs, and most importantly, the eras' roaring music that forever altered the rhythms of the region. My work was to bring these stories to life in the museum space. David's quest was completion of *The Blue Note,* a necessary and honorific documentation of Local 493 musicians.

Our meeting all those years ago was truly a confluence of fate and passion. David was kind enough to allow NAAM to display some of the materials he had collected, including Powell Barnett's Local 493 delegate badge from the 1932 convening of the American Federation of Musicians. In museums, historical objects provide visitors an extraordinary opportunity to connect with our shared past. Powell Barnett's badge offered a portal to a person's life, allowing museum goers to imagine events and ideas that individuals may never have committed to paper. In addition to lending the weight of historic artifacts, David also provided the exhibition with a text panel conveying the importance of Local 493. Important not only to its members, but to our shared understanding of this community's complex past and ongoing evolution.

David's fuller telling of the Seattle's Black Musician's Union story in *The Blue Note* gives readers access to a fascinating moment of Seattle's history, set to the indelible sound of jazz. His work reveals an unlikely convergence of people, places and world events. Dynamic forces swirling together in the centrifuge of a uniquely Northwest experience, transforming our region's cultural landscape. Antiquated liquor laws; an abundance of jobs in wartime industries; an expanding Black community with money to spend; police corruption; booze; gambling and all other manner of vice conspired to make the Northwest a fertile breeding ground for a truly American art form—Jazz. I am eternally grateful this story has been documented and shared.

After my time at NAAM, my career eventually brought me to King County's cultural development authority, 4Culture, where I currently serve as Executive Director. Our team of grant-makers, cultural advocates, advisory committees, and volunteer peer review panelists support a diverse array of cultural endeavors. My job now is to fund, support, and advocate for culture to enhance the quality of life of all King County residents.

On a number of occasions, 4Culture has been able to support David's important research, documentation, and storytelling work. To me, *The Blue Note* is a touchstone and reminder of the of the important work authors, collectors, and public historians provide in interpreting the past. This effort is done so that the collective does not forget, but more critically, so we may use the stories of the past to help us make sense of our present. That is the power of looking back. That is the power of listening to the music and music makers of our past.

Acknowledgments

This book has benefited from the assistance of many people. Background and initial scholarship for the present volume came out of graduate work at Western Washington University in Bellingham, Washington. Thesis advisor Chris Friday originally suggested the topic, and his comments, along with those of Milt Krieger and Rand Jimerson, guided my thesis. Dan Mather, now gone but not forgotten, made tape copies of 78 RPM records by Seattle musicians early on, providing me with a valuable aural research tool. The careful reader will see that I have profited from a detailed reading of Paul de Barros's *Jackson Street After Hours*. Additionally, Paul was helpful with photograph suggestions, shared his interviews, and was enthusiastic about the project from the beginning.

The publication in its present incarnation would not have come about without generous financial assistance provided by back-to-back grants from the King County Landmarks and Heritage Commission. Thanks to that entity's Charles Payton and Holly Taylor for all of their help and belief in this project. After further years, both Debra Twersky and Eric Taylor of 4 Culture stepped in and provided additional suggestions, enthusiastically keeping the project on track.

A hearty thanks to union staff with whom I came in contact during the lengthy research period for this book, particularly Motter Snell, Carol Maxwell and others at the American Federation of Musicians' Union, Local 76-493. After many visits I discovered valuable Local 493 records, uncirculated publications, ads, photographs, and one of a kind memorabilia.

In another life as an agent, I worked extensively with musicians' unions, signing my share of union contracts. In these dealings my attitude ranged from enthusiasm to indifference. And while in this book, Local 76 has taken its share of lumps, the story should not be misconstrued as anti-union. It is very difficult to earn a living as a professional musician and the AFM despite faults, has done more than its share to make that possible.

I am grateful to the institutions which provided research assistance and images. I have made good use of the University of Washington Libraries Special Collections. Now retired archivist Karyl Winn was helpful and zealous initially there. Later U.W. photo archivist Nicolette Bromberg supplied key photographs and clarified rights questions. For this revised edition, invaluable assistance was provided by Conor Casey, Associate Librarian and head of the University's Labor Archives of Washington. I also worked with Casey to transfer all Blue Note research materials to the University archives. At the Seattle Public Library, Valerie Garrett-Turner from the Douglass-Truth branch, and staff at the Fine and Performing Arts department were most helpful. They provided me with the opportunity to discover and use the Ray Charles and Ernestine Anderson stills in their Sotero Collection. Staff at the Ellensburg Public Library assisted with historical information and photographs. Tony Kurtz, then of the Washington State Archives, Central Branch, helped with early Roslyn Washington and union history.

For long distance research assistance, I thank the always merry and bright Tad Hershorn at Rutgers' Institute of Jazz Studies. The Society of American Archivists annual meeting provided an opportunity to interview Frank "Doc" Adams in Birmingham, Alabama. Doc was insightful about the early development of segregated unionism and Seattle's William Funderberg. Author Sherry Tucker helped with International Sweethearts photo and interpretive research. Mary Henry and then Jacqueline E.A. Lawson, both individually and as representatives of the Black Heritage Society of Washington State, provided research help, numerous illustrations, and many clarifications on finer historical points. In the same spirit, Esther Hall Mumford proved to be a valuable resource for interviews and photographs. Howard Giske and other staff at the Museum of History and Industry (MOHAI) were gracious with my photo searches on multiple occasions. Nationally, Bruce Raeburn at the Hogan Jazz Archives of Tulane University, Alfred Lemon and Daniel Hammer at the Historic New Orleans Collection, and Leslie Zlabinger at the Louis Armstrong Archives and House all provided further photographic assistance. Lola Pedrini gets special thanks for providing a rare Quincy Jones big band shot. Ditto to ace photographer Mary Randlett for her work. Scholars Rick Hobbes provided an obscure Cayton family item, and Ken Steiner a great Duke Ellington Seattle find. Frank Driggs was an institution unto himself, and a big help with rare period photographic help.

In the print realm, two institutions gave this project a nice boost when it needed it. I am grateful for an opportunity to publish a portion of this story relating to path-breaking women in *COLUMBIA Magazine* and *BlackPast.org*. Sincere thanks and deep appreciation to editors Christina Orange Dubois and Maria Pascualy at the former, and to Quintard Taylor at the latter. Similarly, Brian Carter and Barbara Earl Thomas at the Northwest African American Museum provided helpful consultations, as well as an opportunity to exhibit Local 493 memorabilia in the "After Hours" exhibit.

The Blue Note would have been impossible without plenty of help from family and friends as well. A tip of the hat to Shelly Parsons, my wife, for a careful read and editing. Thanks too go to Megan and Jack Keller for their understanding of the weekends away and long hours rewriting this story. A big thank you to my parents, Harold and Joanne Keller, for solace and shelter along the I-5 corridor. Ditto to first cousin Steve Evavold, his gracious wife Rae Pearson, along with Carlos, also in jazz heaven, and Bonnie Palmer. They provided places to stay in Seattle along the research trail. A tip of my hat to Manny Keller-Scholz for long distance historical research. For a place to reside while researching in Tacoma, a big thank you to my sister Nancy Keller-Scholz and her husband Rick. During the final stages of manuscript preparation, Milt Krieger offered several useful historical leads. Tari Parsons provided much-appreciated technical acumen and help. Particular thanks as well go to Jerry Wood for production resources. The manuscript also benefitted from Mimi Melnick's eagle-eye in constructing the book's Index.

Musicians and others unselfishly gave of their time, allowing me to interview them and to copy personal photographs and other memorabilia. Since these individuals were elderly when I first made my initial contacts, many of them are now gone. To their families I extend condolences as well as my heartfelt appreciation. Without them this account would not have that first person feel, of which I am particularly proud.

First and foremost in this category is the extended Barnett clan. Doug Barnett, along with James "Smitty" Smith, Helen Smith, and Karen Smith Surall were most helpful during interviews. Doug particularly proved to be a tireless champion of this book, reviewing early drafts of the manuscript, providing useful suggestions and insights. Additionally, I am pleased to acknowledge Dorothy Laigo Cordova, Frank and Don Osias, and Ben Laigo for help in researching Seattle's multi-ethnic music scene, and the Filipino "gray area" as Frank Osias so aptly put it. Other key interviewees graciously provided me with their stories, memories, and/or photographs. These included: Norm Bobrow, Francis Demisse, Roy Green, Dorothy Hilbert, Viola Howell, Zenobia Jefferson, Beverly Kelly, Dorothy Lomax, Dan Mather, Al Smith, Al Turay, and Gerald "Wig" Wiggins.

Finally, I salute the following Local 493 musicians with whom I was able to directly speak. All of them welcomed me into their homes and spoke at great length with me about a time when they made their livings as union musicians and representatives. These were: Kenny Boas, Buddy Catlett, Ralph Davis, William Funderberg, Elmer Gill, Ernie Hatfield, Floyd Standifer, Jabo Ward, and John Willis.

Introduction

This is a story about the hopes and dreams of a small group of African American men and women. They ran their own union in Seattle beginning in the early 1900s. This union was the American Federation of Musicians' Union Local 493. Its members had a dream that they should be able to play their own brand of jazz music and receive a fair wage for this service. They should be able to elect their own leaders, control their own territory, and run their business from their own headquarters.

Such an idea placed them in direct conflict with the dominant white players of Seattle's music establishment. It also ensured that their journey would not be an easy one. It is a musical tale filled with woe, but it is also a powerful story that uplifts with its sheer dogged determination. And it swings.

The Blue Note is a sort of David and Goliath pictorial history. It involves a small band of thirty to one hundred determined African American union musicians who tried to control part of their destiny in work-a-day Seattle. First in 1918 with the American Federation of Musicians' (AFM) Local 458, and then in 1924 with Local 493 the union became an institution. These humble beginnings were at a shared meeting space at the 2024 Fourth Avenue headquarters of the powerful white musicians' Local 76 under decidedly Jim Crow conditions. Later during much of the 1930s and 1940s its space was at the home of 493's President Gerald Wells. From the early 1950s until amalgamation in 1956, Local 493 operated from a modest one-room business office. Here the fabled "Blue Note," as the club house style local was known, operated dispensing union justice and its own brand of union culture. Located at 1319 East Jefferson, it took care of business, held swinging after-hours jam sessions with famous out of town ringers, served patrons up a cool taste at a full bar, and took in all comers who wanted to be part of a more relaxed and fraternal musical endeavor.

This chapter of our shared cultural history is now a dim memory. Most of the men and women who were around during this time are gone. Yet their photographs and memorabilia bring alive a special time. It was an era when blacks were not on a level playing field with whites. This must have been particularly galling in the entertainment fields, despite the often superior strengths of "race" musicians. In an early, and rare successful effort to better themselves and to control a portion of their economic destiny, Seattle's black musicians organized their own union. Politically cunning union musicians such as "Yellow Dog Democrat" Powell Barnett, Charles Adams, Virginia Hughes, and Leon Jackson, among others lead this effort.

The stories in *The Blue Note* can remind and inspire us about past achievements. The segregated musicians of Local 493 faced long odds and survived for almost 30 years. Overcoming prejudice and discriminatory interpretations of union law frequently laid down by the "parent," white local 76, a resilient group of jazz musicians held their own. Specifically, they controlled their own turf, established and adhered to the AFM union pay scale, and, when necessary, disciplined their own members.

Along the way they seem to have had fun. When it came to matters of music and race, Local 493 was miles ahead of its mother local. Trumpeter, composer, educator, and 493 union stalwart, Floyd Standifer, recalled that Local 76 officials would have let jazz and bebop music die. He recalled these officials maintaining that black musicians "were just playing a bunch of wrong notes."

Another lasting contribution of the American Federation of Musicians' Local 493 was that it took in all interested parties. Beginning in the 1930s, white bassist Bill Rinaldi gave up on the white musicians' local and joined African American 493. Other Caucasian musicians including Mike DeFillipis and Kenny Boas opted out of the white union. They preferred a non-old-boy system, where they were free to play jazz and jam in a more relaxed atmosphere. Such inclusive practices, prompted Standifer to refer to his union as a "Rainbow Coalition." Strengthening this claim is the fact that in addition to Caucasian members, both Hawaiian and Hispanic surnamed individuals were also 493 union members.

Today we are beginning to embrace the practices of inclusion and diversity. The stories here remind us that this process has been a long, complicated, and problem-filled one. Yet these stories and their accompanying images are also hopeful for the accomplishments and joyful camaraderie they celebrate. These stories inspire. And, if you cock your head just right you'll begin to hear as well as feel the music and spirit of a special era when things began to change.

That said, what this volume strives to provide is a look at a largely untold story of jazz, race, and unionism. Within its covers you'll see photographs of and read about lesser known locals, as well as "name" players from early jazz times through the swing era and on into the heady days of bebop. To the necromancers of this art, those undersung, black, brown, and white musicians who were all members of the American Federation of Musicians' Union Locals 458 and 493, this one's for you.

The Blue Note

The story of Seattle's segregated unions begins far away from the city. The father of one of its key organizers was Powell Barnett, Sr., shown here at about 39 years old. In 1888 he journeyed west by train from Brazil, Indiana for a job as a miner, with his family. Barnett, Sr., along with others from Ohio, Illinois, and Indiana, were enticed to journey west for work. Recruited by an African American contractor and saloon owner named James E. Shepperson, the Barnett family eventually came to a small town nestled in the Cascade Mountains named Roslyn, Washington. There armed guards met them and issued each male head of household a rifle for protection. Unknown to Barnett and the other African American miners on this train, they initially served as strikebreakers in a conflict between the Knights of Labor and the Northern Pacific Coal Company. This newfound work was in the small mining towns of Roslyn and Ronald or "Number Three," as the latter was also called. By and by these black miners integrated into the community, becoming unionized in 1904 by the militant United Federation of Miners. They also joined various churches and other social organizations such as the black Masons, Knights of Tabor, and the Knights of Pythia for men and the Eastern Star and Daughters of the Tabernacle for women. The activities of these organizations included various "social events, dances, balls, and picnics." These brought about an eventual interaction between three groups of miners "Slavonia people," others of European extraction, and African Americans. Among the Barnett family was a five-year old Powell Barnett, Jr., who would go on to become a founder of Seattle's first black musicians' union, the American Federation of Musicians' Local 458.

1.) Powell Barnett, Sr. circa 1895, in Roslyn, Washington.
Photo courtesy Ellensburg Public Library.

This photo shows a teen-aged Powell Barnett, Jr. with his tuba in the attire of the Roslyn community military band. The Northwest Improvement Company coal mining group allowed blacks and other ethnic miners their own distinct bands and helped each purchase uniforms and instruments. However, musician and miner Barnett chafed at company ultimatums which stopped the white music instructor from providing lessons to him. Additionally, Barnett grew weary of company town strictures, particularly when the black mine foreman and recruiting agent, James E. Shepperson, squelched an attempt by blacks to build their own club house and practice space.

2.) Young Powell Barnett, Jr. in Roslyn band uniform early 1900s.
Photo courtesy *The Seattle Medium.*

One of the Roslyn Marching Brass Bands is shown here. This all black band may have been named Payne's Military Band, which is written on the bass drum. Powell Barnett performed in a similar band, although he had left the area by this time. After six years of work in the coal mines in and around Roslyn, at 22 Barnett moved to Seattle to seek his fortune in 1906. Barnett recalled his brass band activity fondly, stating that the band "flourished" and played "different events in town: the Sunday school, churches, lodges, and what-have-you, just like the other bands did."

3.) Roslyn Marching Brass Band, circa 1920.
Photo courtesy Ellensburg Public Library.

This image depicts an African American "forty-five piece stage band from the South" at the Alaska-Yukon-Pacific Exposition in 1909. The bass drumhead reads, "The Great Dixieland Spectacle-Lacy's Band."

From 1900 to 1910 Seattle's black population grew from 406 to 2,296 during a period of rapid development. During this same era the total city population tripled from 80,671 to 237,194. Such growth provided work for many, including the eventual musicians' union leader Powell Barnett. Barnett landed one of his first musical jobs as a tuba player in a practice band rehearsing for a part in Exposition festivities, some of which took place at the Dixieland Theatre.

4.) Lacy's Dixieland Band during the Alaska-Yukon-Pacific Exposition at the Dixieland Theatre in Seattle, 1909. Photo courtesy Special Collections Division University of Washington Libraries, Photo by Nowell, Negative No. 1846.

Tuba man Powell Barnett integrates the Volunteers of America Marching Band opposite. During the years 1909-1914 Barnett played regularly with this band "at 825 23rd Avenue and on Pioneer Square." With Seattle being a heavily unionized town at the time, this work with the Volunteers band brought Barnett into the white American Federation of Musicians' (AFM) Union Local 76 in December of 1913. As early as 1908 Barnett tried to convince other black musicians to join Seattle's Local 76. Interestingly enough the white local, which was formed on March 1, 1893, stated in its Constitution that "All instrumental performers who are citizens of the United States or Canada... shall be eligible for membership," and honored its charter when Barnett became the first and only African American to join the otherwise lily-white union. After this, the tuba man stayed busy during World War I, founding and playing tuba in another marching band. Associated with the paramilitary Tenth Division Patriotic Defense Council, the thirty-member, all-black band helped march new soldiers "from Second and Virginia to the King Street (train) depot" during the war. The band attracted a following for such efforts and eventually, after lengthy labor wrangles, went on in 1925 to play in city parks department concerts.

Barnett along with a group of unrecorded other musicians successfully began the process of petitioning for a union on August 9th, 1918, and Seattle's first segregated musicians' union, AFM Local 458, was born. Only one month before the Seattle General Strike of February 6 - 11, 1919, there is a direct reference to "Bro Barnett," and in January of 1919 "Local 458 (Colored)" was successfully organized. Barnett remained a life-long union musician with Local 76 and maintained dual membership status from 1918-1956 in both the black and white musicians' unions. He was the only African American to do so during this lengthy period. Other black musicians whose names appear in early union Board correspondence or notes include: President Charles Adams, R.H. McCurdy Secretary, Leon Jackson, S.L. Murray, Virginia M. Hughes, Mr. Dominick, Bro Bates, (Edythe and Floyd) Turnham, Lucien B. Fields, Henry Campbell, J.J. Stanbrough, Henry Allen, Mr. Johnson, and Mrs. Austin and Mrs. Gertrude H. Wright.

5.) Powell Barnett with the Volunteers of America Marching Band, circa 1911.
Photo courtesy of Karen Smith Surall collection.

The Whang Doodle Orchestra, formally depicted here, was one of Seattle's first jazz bands. The group kept busy in the era, playing in 1918 at the Woodmen of the World or W.O.W. lodge and at Levy's Orpheum. Music patriarch Frank Waldron was an early member of the just formed black musicians' union, AFM Local 458, and must have understood such union rules as playing for scale. However, the band got into a scrape with Local 76, while working around town. Among other offenses, the parent, white union charged that the Whang Doodle Orchestra worked under scale at the W.O.W. lodge. Waldron, shown with trumpet, was also a noted alto saxophonist, composer, and music instructor, who became a member of Local 493 as well. He went on to influence generations of Seattle musicians including Dick Wilson, Buddy Catlett, Ron Pierce, Jabo Ward, and Quincy Jones among others, all of whom took weekly lessons from Waldron.

6.) Whang Doodle Orchestra, circa 1915-1918. Left to right: Mr. Hughes, mandolin; Ace Brooks, mandolin; unknown; Frank Waldron, trumpet; and Coty Jones, piano. Photo courtesy of Esther Hall Mumford.

Ferdinand "Jelly Roll" Morton played in and around Seattle and the Pacific Northwest from 1919-1921, using Local 458 musicians on more than one occasion. Morton stayed with Bessie Johnson a.k.a. Anita Gonzales, the owner of a boarding house in Tacoma, which he used as his home base during these years. The self-styled "inventor of jazz" described Ms. Gonzales as the only woman he ever really loved and the only one who ever "managed" him. The bandleader spent five years on the West Coast from 1917-1922, residing much of the time in and around Los Angeles, but also worked in Tijuana, San Diego, and San Francisco. In the Northwest, Mr. Jelly Lord did not yet possess the reputation he was to gain with his Red Hot Peppers, (see ad opposite.) Morton at 28 years old when he came north, was a seasoned vaudevillian. Just hitting his stride then as a pianist and composer, he'd also worked as a gambler, would-be pool hustler, and pimp. Anita, a sharp businesswoman, helped bankroll him for extended periods during his West Coast days. She had just made a large amount of money running a Las Vegas saloon called The Arcade in a wide open area called "Block 16," where prostitution also flourished.

Morton may have played Seattle in June 1920, and on July 31, 1920 was on his way to a gig at Seattle's Entertainer's Club at 12th Avenue South and Main Street. Others recall him playing elsewhere in town. So, it is probably safe to say that he performed in Seattle at least once and may have played other undocumented Seattle shows as well. Confirmed dates are in Vancouver, British Columbia, where he paid dues as a traveling member of that city's American Federation of Musicians' Union Local 145, (and then quickly took the money back in February of 1921.) For this Vancouver appearance he is listed as playing "with Eubanks, Hall, and others from Local 458 (Seattle, colored.)" Morton played first at a cabaret in Vancouver and then at the Regent Hotel. Horace Eubanks, was described by Morton as "A beautiful hot clarinet from East St. Louis, who learned from New Orleans men." Later in 1923 in Chicago, Eubanks also recorded "Jazz Band" and "Steamboat" with Morton for Okeh. Additionally, the Vancouver unit featured Doc Hutchinson, "a drummer from Baltimore." Jelly also played Portland, Oregon on or about 31 July 1920, and though no evidence has yet surfaced, probably played Tacoma during this time too. In Vancouver he worked in an octet at Will Bowman's Patricia Café in September 1919, at the Regent there in late 1920 or early 1921, and at Patty Sullivan's Club in February of 1921. At the Patricia Café, Jelly Roll claimed to be the leader of the band. However, Seattle resident, music patriarch, and Local 458 member Oscar Holden, who was originally from Nashville and Chicago, is listed as the band leader in published sources. Giving strength to Holden's claim is the fact that he worked at the Patricia for more than a year, while the hot-headed Morton was there only one or two months. Morton then pushed on from Vancouver to Casper, Wyoming. The one thing that is certain during this time is that Jelly Roll was gambling and losing large amounts of money in Vancouver and Seattle. This experience was eventually documented in a Morton composition, "Seattle Hunch," which, while probably written earlier, has a copyright date of September 28, 1929.

7.) The Originator – Jelly Roll Morton, circa 1927. Courtesy of The Historic New Orleans Collection, accession number 2000-17-L.1.

Gertrude Harvey Wright was an early and rare female member of Seattle's first black musicians' union, Local 458. Among a select few women unionists for this period, other 458 members who can be positively identified were Edythe Turnham, a "Mrs. Austin," who became the unions' first female officer in 1931, and Virginia Hughes. Other women musicians who worked regularly with Local 458 men, and who, thus, could have been union members, include the previously depicted Coty Jones, along with Lillian Smith, Freda Shaw (who worked cruise ships with Joe Darensbourg et al), Evelyn Bundy, Lillian Goode, Zelma Winslow, and Evelyn Williamson. Pianist Wright is shown here at 32 years old. By this time, she had already played in various bands, including some with Frank Waldron and trombonist Robert McCurdy in and around mountain towns such as Gold Bar, Washington. She figures in the battle to save the local in January and February 1924. According to union documents, Local 458 was in dire straits and had particularly incensed its "mother union," Local 76 when 458 dissidents wrote a critical letter to the International, disputing various infractions, questioning 76's authority and labeling Barnett a "hypocrite." Wright, along with 458 members R.H. McCurdy, Charles Adams, Leon Jackson, and S.L. Murray mollified 76 by writing another letter to the International stating that the earlier missive "did not represent the consensus of opinion of Local 458."

However, in April 1924, Seattle's black musicians' union Local 458 had its charter revoked at the recommendation of white Local 76. This came about due to 458's holding illegal elections in 1921, and for its failure to follow 76's working rules book and price list, and for basically not functioning for at least 2 years. During these troubled times, Charles Adams and Powell Barnett were Local 458's presidents, while R.H. McCurdy was its secretary. Two years later McCurdy was summarily dismissed by Local 76 for financial improprieties, although he steadfastly refused to acknowledge the white union's power over his actions and "refused to be tried by any other than his own local." Thanks to the diplomatic skills of Powell Barnett, eight months later Seattle's black musicians were granted their own union, albeit under tighter 76 strictures. A new American Federation of Musicians' Local 493, received a charter from the International in December 1924, when membership was listed at 35, a figure that would grow to 55 six months later. By way of contrast, average membership in Local 76 during this same period was 1200.

8.) Gertrude Harvey Wright, circa 1920. Photo courtesy Jacqueline E. A. Lawson.

Not everyone was pleased with the progress being made in 1922 by Seattle's black union members. Here, AFM Local 76 member Lue Vernon takes racist swipes at music played by black musicians in Madison Park. Vernon unflatteringly compares them to the white marching musicians of Wagner's Band, a local institution and crowd favorite. As early as June 1915, Vernon had published other racist poetry in the *International Musician*. In defense of "Dad" or "Pop" Wagner, this president of Local 76 in the 1920s presided over one of the earliest attempts to integrate the two unions.

While this poem highlights Seattle period racism, jazz music was viewed negatively by white International officials as well. A notable example of this appears in the Local 76 newspaper, *Musicland,* where International Vice President W.L. Mayer penned a 1922 cover story attack on "Jazz Maniacs" deploring their "musical immorality." Neither was black Seattle's bourgeoisie particularly fond of jazz. In a 1920 article Madge Cayton described jazz as "the delirium tremens of syncopation." She went on to warn that the "the alluring god of jazz, Mumbo Jumbo" could lead to a failure to appreciate "the real god of music, Pan... the real classic." She concluded however, by labeling jazz as a "necessary evil." One of the locals playing "evil" jazz of only a few years later in 1926 and 1927, was drummer and singer Leonard Gayton, who co-led the popular Garfield Ramblers band around town with pianist Evelyn Bundy.

WAGNER'S BAND

Luk yer, Nigger, stop yo' talkin'
'Bout dem "crack bands" in de South,
Fo' I'se tired ob dem ole chess'nuts
Comin' from yo' possum mouth.
Yo' all time spout ob "Liberatti,"
"Innes,"
The "Iowa State" and "Gilmore's"
band
But by golly, "Wagner's" Regiment
Am de "Boss-ox" ob dis land.

To Madison Park ebery Sunday
Dis yer coon jes shuffles out
Fo' to hear de "Darkies Tickle,"
An' to hear de chil'run shout,
Fo' de ladies an' de babies
An' de sweethearts han' in han',
Begin dancing, singing, ragging
When dey hears "Dad" Wagner's band.

Yo' may talk about yo' palm trees,
Far away in Georgia lan'
Whar yo' sit 'neath tropic shub'ry
While alistenin' to de band.
But here, Nigger, in Seattle
Whar de silver salmons grow,
De boys doan club mosquitors
When playin' "Ambolena Snow."

Don't tell me ob yo' crack-bands
Fo' we's up to snuff out here.
'Cause we hears de latest music
When de "Regiment" does appear.
An' dose lubly summer concerts
Lord! I hopes dey'll come agen,
So I drinks good health to Wagner,
Kind regards to all his men.

Den, luk here, Nigger, stop yo' talkin'
'Bout dem "crack-bands" in de South,
Fo' I'se tired ob dem ole chess-nuts
Comin' frum yo' possum mouth.
Yo' all time spout ob "Liberatti,"
"Innes,"
De "Iowa State" an' "Gilmore's" band,
But by golly, "Wagners" Regiment
Am de "boss-ox" ob dis lan'.
    LUE F. VERNON.
    * * *

9.) "Wagner's Band" poem. Originally published in *Musicland* magazine in Seattle June 15, 1922. Reprint courtesy of American Federation of Musicians' Union Local 76-493.

Bandleader and pianist Edythe Turnham, nee Edith Payne, was originally from Topeka, Kansas. In August 1907 she married drummer Floyd Turnham in Spokane where Floyd worked as a waiter at the Spokane Club. They were both 21. Two years later they had a son, Floyd, Jr., who would grow up to play clarinet and all the saxophones in his mother's bands. He later attended Garfield High, where he met up with Jimmy and Wayne Adams and Creon Thomas of the Garfield Ramblers, along with other Garfield jazz musicians. Floyd, Jr. also studied in Seattle with Frank Waldron, and went on to eventual fame in Los Angeles where his 1939 band "became the nucleus" for Les Hite's 1940 big band. Floyd, Jr. also was a stalwart with the bands of Gerald Wilson, Count Basie, and Teddy Wilson among others. Edythe worked in vaudeville as part of a family minstrel troupe during the 1910s with her younger sister, Maggie, touring Eastern Washington and Idaho. The Turnhams remained in Spokane until 1920. The family moved first from Spokane to Tacoma in 1920, and then around 1922 to Seattle.

Edythe, husband Floyd, Sr., and son Floyd, Jr., formed the nucleus of one of Seattle's important early bands. The band started off in 1922 as a quintet with sister Maggie as an added attraction as an entertainer and dancer. In 1926 the band also included Powell Samuel Barnett playing the bass line on tuba, then the fashion, along with Dave Hendricks on tenor saxophone, Charles Adams on trumpet, and Babe Hackley on banjo. Her big band was originally billed as The Knights of Syncopation and in 1928 as The Black Hawks Orchestra and was active on the Seattle scene. As a Local 493 member, Turnham was on both sides of musicians' union conflicts as well. In 1926, she successfully charged that her band had been undercut by Morgan Jackson and his Black Satin Orchestra from the cruise ship, *H.F. Alexander,* at a dance given by the Colored Elks at Renton Hall. The following year in 1927, her band was accused of "working on day off." The Black Hawks photo and story appeared in Local 76's newspaper, *Musicland,* in 1928. Their white manager, John Dallavo, a 76 member and composer, booked them on an Orpheum Circuit international tour from "Winnipeg to Long Beach," which included a week's run at Seattle's Orpheum Theatre. In 1932 "Edythe Turnham And Her Plantation Syncopators" played at The Plantation, just north of the Seattle city limits. During this same time, Edythe and family played the Club Alabam on fabled Central Avenue in Los Angeles with a ten-piece band billed as "Edythe Turnham and Her Dixie Aces." The family stayed on in Southern California, and Ms. Turnham continued to work there until 1945.

10.) Edythe Turnham Five, c. 1923. L-R: Floyd Turnham Sr.; unknown; Edythe; Floyd Turnham, Jr.; and Charles Adams. Photo courtesy Black Heritage Society of Washington State, Inc.

11.) Edythe Turnham Orchestra, c. 1926-27. L-R: H.A. Jones; Charles Adams; Floyd Turnham, Sr.; Boone; Edythe Turnham; Eddie "Fats" Wilson; Floyd Turnham, Jr.; Bruce Rowell. Photo courtesy of Dorothy Hilbert. **Black Hawks in 1928 ad, L-R: Joe Bailey; Crawford Brown; Ray Williams; Floyd Turnham, Sr.; Floyd Turnham, Jr.; Robert Taylor; Floyd Wilson; Creon Thomas; and Edythe Turnham seated.** Courtesy of AFM Local 76-493.

Local 493 man Frank Waldron appears again here, switching to alto saxophone with the Odeon Jazz Orchestra circa mid-1920s. One of Seattle's first generation of jazz performers – a master of both trumpet and sax – Waldron was also an influential music instructor to decades of younger musicians. The multi-talented musician composed and published music as well. Among his compositions are "Climb Them Walls," "Low Down," "With Pep," and "Valse Maguerite." These and other songs appear in his *Syncopated Classic* saxophone method book, published and copyrighted in 1924 by the Waldron School of Saxophone and Trumpet, located at 1242 Jackson Street.

This photograph, which appears to be at the Nanking Café, indicates a classic jazz line up. The Odeon Jazz Orchestra's engagement at the café, which was at 1616½ Fourth Avenue, is an interesting color line development. Previously, downtown Seattle had been off limits to most black musicians, who generally played the smaller and less desirable clubs bordered by Madison Avenue. The engagement reflects positively on bandleader Waldron's savvy business skills and shows his stature in both the white and black music and union worlds. Further evidence of such skills came in 1925 when this "Nanking Orchestra" successfully defended itself as a 493 union band, refuting a Local 76 charge of working seven consecutive days at the restaurant.

12.) The Odeon Jazz Orchestra at the Nanking Café, circa mid-1920s, L-R: Frank Waldron, alto saxophone; trumpet, unknown; Archie Jackson, piano; trombone: unknown; Ralph Stevens or Ralph Gibbs, drums. Photo courtesy Black Heritage Society of Washington State, Inc.

This ad is for an appearance of a quartet led by Jimmy Adams at the "Shanghai Restaurants." The two venues were located "opposite the Smith Building" at 711 Pike Street, with another at 100 2nd Avenue, near Yesler. In this mid-1920s ad, the businesses had a policy of "snappy jazz." They also invited customers "to eat while you dance," a gastronomically challenging proposition.

Jimmy Adams was a trumpet playing 493 man and a relative of organizer and fellow trumpeter Charles Adams. During this period Adams worked in various combos with his brother and fellow Garfield High School alum Wayne Adams on saxophones. While at Garfield the brothers were part of the well-regarded Garfield Ramblers, which was organized by fellow 493 members, pianist Evelyn Bundy, and drummer Leonard Gayton. Jimmy Adams played throughout the region, including at Tacoma's Valhalla Hall for a 1926 show, where the playbill advertised "Honey Dip" by Jimmy Adams' Candy Kids. The Adams brothers were stalwarts in the early Seattle jazz world, playing professionally with local pianist Creon Thomas in various bands including those of famed New Orleans clarinetist Joe Darensbourg, who first came to a wide-open Seattle on the cruise ship *H.F. Alexander* in 1928. The Shanghai Restraurants must have featured black bands for some time, since, also in 1928, 493 members were in a dispute with their parent local, white 76, for working the cafes with a non-union (and white) musician. Ten years later both Jimmy and brother Wayne stayed busy and earned great wages in the considerably less restrictive club atmosphere of Shanghai, China. There they played in various bands including that of fellow Local 493 man, Earl Whaley.

13.) Jimmy Adams Collegiate 4 at Shanghai Restaurants, circa 1926. Ad courtesy of University of Washington Libraries, Manuscripts, and Special Collections, University Archives.

The publicity still opposite shows Mamie Smith & Her Jazz Hounds circa 1923. It is inscribed to black Seattle entrepreneur Russell ("Noodles") Smith at his Golden West Hotel, located at 710 Seventh Avenue South in Seattle's International District. The photo hints at an appearance by Smith's band in Seattle during this time. While newspaper or other print references to such an appearance are inconclusive, early area residents Bruce Rowell and Emma Gayton maintained that both Mamie Smith and Bessie Smith performed in town during this time.

Mamie Smith is immortalized in jazz history for making "Crazy Blues" on August 10, 1920, the first blues hit record by a female black artist. The 78 RPM Okeh disc also featured "That Thing Called Love." Originally the Okeh session was to have been done by the white Broadway singer, Sophie Tucker. However, when Tucker became ill, the persuasive Perry Bradford talked Okeh's white recording director Ralph Peer into letting Smith record. On both tunes Smith was backed by The Rega Orchestra, a white band. These songs followed an earlier successful session in February 1920 where Smith recorded songwriter and her pianist Perry Bradford's "You Can't Keep A Good Man Down." "Crazy Blues" was also written by Bradford, with "It's Right Here for You" on the flip side. The song was an immediate hit, and quickly sold a million and a half copies for Okeh records at a then hefty $1 a disc. Bradford, the rare black musician and songwriter who held on to his composer's royalties, on this song received $53,000 in residuals. Seattle musicians and black residents no doubt purchased this first big hit record as well, helping to popularize the powerful singer. Smith toured extensively during this period; her name made well known through her records. In addition to the blues and jazz vocalist, also depicted in this photograph and identifiable, is a fresh-faced, 19 year-old Coleman Hawkins on tenor saxophone, who remained in the band from 1922 until after a 1923 West Coast tour with Smith. James "Bubber" Miley, who went on to star in Duke Ellington's band until 1929, is on cornet, and song writer and publisher Perry Bradford is at the piano.

14.) Mamie Smith & Her Jazz Hounds at Seattle's Golden West Hotel, circa 1923.
Fourth from right holding cornet James Wesley "Bubber" Miley, next is Coleman Hawkins, Smith, and Perry Bradford at piano. Autographed Smith presentation photograph by Apeda. Courtesy of the Black Heritage Society of Washington State.

Whether or not Bessie Smith, "Empress of the Blues," appeared in Seattle during the early 1920s is unfortunately obscured by the mists of time. However, Smith's impact on Seattle's budding jazz scene was clearly felt through film and her records. Not an overnight recording success, Bessie struggled to find a company that believed in her. She was turned down by Okeh, and others during this same era, including Thomas Edison, who marked her record audition as "n.g." for no good. Her fortune changed when Columbia invested in her, with whom she made more than 150 songs from 1923 to 1933 including "Taint Nobody's Business" and "Down Hearted Blues;" the latter would sell more than 750,000 copies. In the world of film, she would only make one movie. Shown here is a reproduction of a poster for this appearance. It was in a 1929 Warner Brothers' short film entitled *St. Louis Blues,* directed by Dudley Murphy, with the script co-authored by W. C. Handy. Handy was also the music director for the picture, which featured most of the Fletcher Henderson big band, along with stride piano giant James P. Johnson. Smith's 16-minute, two-reel short film appearance, featuring an all black cast, must have made for a thrilling experience for Emerald City's black movie patrons, who were already fans of hers through her records of five and six years earlier.

A substantial number of early films featured jazz soundtracks and continued to help bring this music to cities across the land. Although Al Jolson's melodramatic 1927 outing in blackface, *The Jazz Singer,* is generally credited as the first jazz vehicle and the first "talking picture," more authentic jazz movies could also be viewed by Seattle area audiences. The list was long and featured: Eddie Peabody in *Banjomania,* a 1927 seven-minute Vitaphone Music short; The Cruise Brothers' *The Missouri Sheiks,* another 1927 nine-minute Vitaphone short with the brothers playing John Handy's "Beale St. Blues," along with "Turkey in the Straw," and others, like "Syncopating Sensation," "Banjoland," and "Strum Fun" all by Peabody. A full length film the same year, King Vidor's highly successful, all-black MGM 1929 production, *Hallelujah!,* featured the Curtis Mosby Orchestra, a.k.a. the Kansas City Blue Blowers. *Bundle of Blues,* another great film from this era was released in 1933 as an eight-minute Paramount Studios short and featured the Duke Ellington Orchestra.

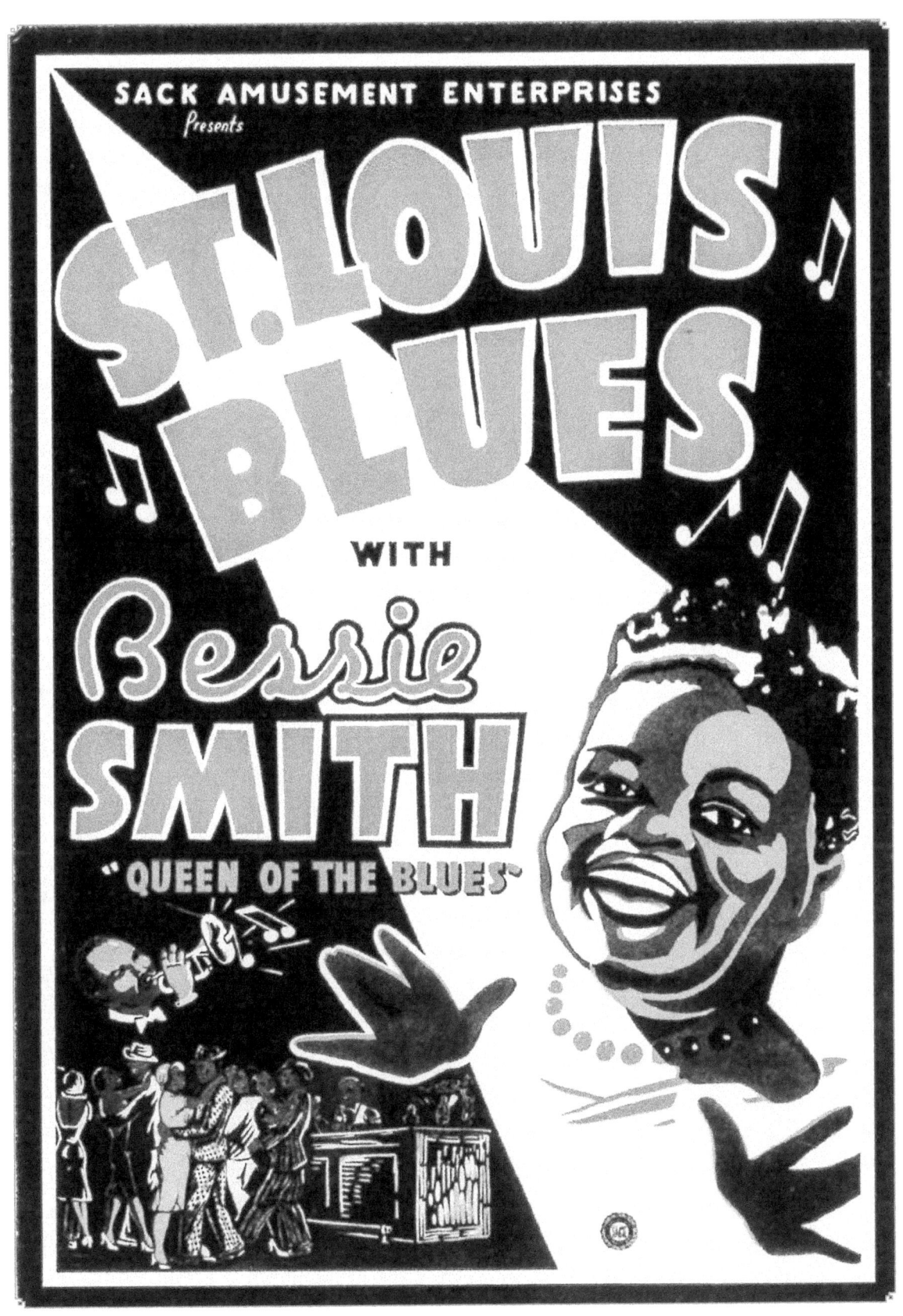

15.) Bessie Smith in *St. Louis Blues,* **film short, Sack Amusement Enterprises, 1929.**
Image from author's collection.

In addition to being one of the first musicians to make use of the new film medium to enhance his popularity, banjo virtuoso and showman Eddie Peabody was also an early and prolific recording artist. Beginning in 1925 he recorded for the Gennett, Banner, Domino and Silvertone labels amongst others. He also increased his popularity through frequent coast-to-coast, NBC radio appearances. Surviving filmed performances indicate that he was master of the plectrum banjo, who favored a repertoire of jazz and vaudeville material which made him popular with U.S. audiences.

Here the musician is shown in an ad from 1927 and is billed as the "Banjoy Boy of Joyland." The copy also refers to him as a "Victor Recording and Vitaphone Artist" indicating the power of the medium, which would continue to help build audiences for jazz throughout Seattle and the rest of the country. Set to play Loew's State Theatre in Los Angeles next in early 1928, Peabody was no stranger to the Pacific Northwest. Regionally, he had just played around the opening of the Mt. Baker Theater in Bellingham in 1927. Indeed, he (or his record company,) must have been on a winning streak when he purchased this full-page, holiday greeting in the Local 76 newspaper, *Musicland*. He also played Seattle's Fifth Avenue Theater in April of the following year. For such appearances, Peabody helped bolster the powerful, white American Federation of Musicians' union Local 76 when he paid his travelling dues.

16.) Eddie Peabody, 1927. Advertising *Musicland* special edition December 1927.
Courtesy of AFM Local 76-493.

Shown in this 1930 newspaper clip, Charles "Tiny" Burnett, a stalwart of white Local 76, hams it up with famed band leader Paul Whiteman in Seattle for an April performance, which introduced many Seattleites to jazz. Whiteman was born in Denver, Colorado and had worked extensively in that city from 1910 - 1920, as well as in San Francisco and Los Angeles, first playing in symphonies and then leading his own orchestras. Whiteman had a big hit with his 1920 recording "Whispering," with a B side of "Japanese Sandman" for Victor, which sold 1.25 million copies in five years. A high point in his career combining classical and jazz musics occurred in 1924. At New York City's Aeolian Hall, he debuted George Gershwin's "Rhapsody in Blue," featuring Gershwin playing piano. Crowned as the "King of Jazz," due to a successful press campaign and a Universal Studios 1930 film of the same name, he helped make jazz popular with mainstream, white concert-going audiences. In the late 1920s he tried to hire black musicians like his friend Eubie Blake. When his manager nixed this practice, Whiteman eventually traded arrangements with black bandleader Fletcher Henderson. Whiteman also hired a young William Grant Still who became "his most prolific songwriter," notably in 1930 when the multi-talented African American composer orchestrated for Whiteman's KFI weekly "Old Gold Hour" radio shows in Los Angeles.

His large orchestra featured some of the leading musicians and improvisers of the day, including the Dorsey brothers, Bix Beiderbecke, Frankie Trumbauer, and Eddie Lang. The band was also respected by both black and white musicians for arrangements, which "were marvels of orchestrational ingenuity." Another member of Whiteman's band from 1929 to 1930, was Joe Venuti, the "world's greatest jazz violinist" and inveterate practical joker, who become a Seattle resident in the early 1960s after gigs and visits in the late 1950s. Though disparaged by some for an early, bombastic style, and a "semi-classical repertoire or vaudeville variety," Whiteman was anything but a harsh task master and kept Bix Beiderbecke's chair open when Bix was too ill to make engagements. Of the bandleader, Venuti once remarked, "Don't ever make fun of Paul Whiteman. He took pride in having the finest musicians in the world and paid the highest salaries ever paid." The band, which played Seattle around April of 1930, probably included Venuti, as well as Washington State residents Bing Crosby and Al Rinker from Spokane, and Mildred Bailey, nee Rinker – Al's sister, originally from Tekoa.

"Tiny" Burnett is included here as an example of how the other half, a.k.a. white Local 76 unionists, lived. In 1907 Burnett played "strictly Viennese music" and "knocked 'em dead with Sol Levi's 'Naughty Waltz'" at the old Butler Hotel, receiving $25 a week for his efforts. The pianist and band leader went on to lead the orchestra at The Alhambra in 1917 for various silent films, including the D.W. Griffith feature, *Intolerance*. Burnett was hailed as the "most popular band leader on the old Orpheum Circuit" at Seattle's Moore Theater during vaudeville times. All such crème de la crème jobs were only available to white members of Local 76, which during the 1920s had at least 610 steadily working musicians out of a total membership of 1200. The much smaller black Local 493 musicians were not allowed into this well-paying concert music world. Indeed, not until 1968 did the Seattle Symphony Orchestra hire African American bassist Bruce Lawrence, and this only after Douglas Q. Barnett, son of Powell S. Barnett, helped to wage a protest campaign against the orchestra's discriminatory hiring practices.

17.) Paul Whiteman, circa 1930 in Seattle with Charles "Tiny" Burnett, pianist, conductor, and lifetime AFM Local 76 member. Newspaper clipping from Special Collections and Preservation Division, University of Washington Libraries.

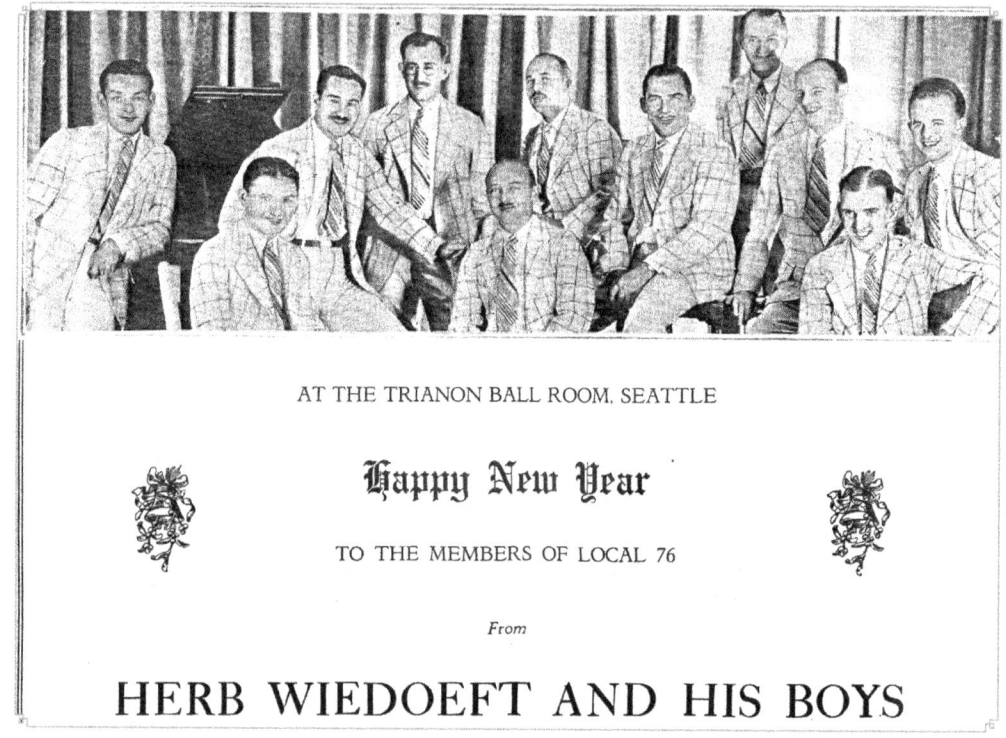

18.) Herb Wiedoeft and His Boys, Christmas 1927 from *Musicland* holiday supplement. Courtesy American Federation of Musicians' Union Local 76-493.

Here are two views of society band leader, trumpeter and Local 76 union dues-payer, Herb Wiedoeft and his band. Based by the mid-1920s out of the prestigious Biltmore Hotel in Los Angeles, Wiedoeft's Cinderella Roof Orchestra recorded extensively for Brunswick during the era. He and his band appear on a sheet music cover of "Egyptian Honeymoon" (opposite), and in a Local 76 *Musicland* Christmas ad (above), both from 1927. Wiedoeft came from a musical Detroit family, whose best known member was his brother Rudy a famous, C melody saxophonist who recorded more than 300 sides. Two other brothers, drummer Adolph, and tuba man Gerhardt worked with him and are pictured on the accompanying "Egyptian Honeymoon" cover. In May 1927 Herb Wiedoeft's Orchestra left their steady job at the Biltmore Hotel to open the Trianon Ballroom in Seattle, advertised here in both illustrations. The Trianon stretched a full half block "from Wall Street to Vine Street on Third Avenue." Built by the fast-living proprietor of the Butler Hotel John Savage, Wiedoeft helped finance the effort. "Herb and His Boys" made up one of the dominant West Coast orchestras of the day for syncopated jazz and "sweet" music. Wiedoeft's successful career was cut short when he died May 12, 1928 in an automobile accident near Klamath Falls, Oregon. Trombonist Jesse Stafford took over the band, basing it in San Francisco, where it continued until 1937. "Herb Wiedoeft And His Boys" are a good example of the white hotel orchestras recorded in various cities, which performed in "racially segregated big city hotels and carriage-trade cabarets." Wiedoeft's band also played union-scale radio broadcasts for KFOA, a market controlled by Local 76, along with other venues such as the Trianon. Local 493 members were locked out of both of these lucrative markets.

19.) "Egyptian Honeymoon" arrangement for Herb Wiedoeft's Orchestra at the Trianon, 1927. Sheet music cover from author's collection.

Shown opposite in this Kirwin of Seattle publicity still is the Vic Meyers Orchestra, replete with dancers and vocalists, circa 1928. The popular bandleader and recording artist was a Local 76 stalwart and larger than life Depression-era figure. Beginning in the early 1920s, Meyers played jobs and did live radio broadcasts at venues such as the "notorious" (for its bootleg liquor policies) Rose Room of the Butler Hotel. This was a great gig for whites, but generally off limits to the black musicians in Local 493, even though the Butler's waiters were all black. The hard drinking Meyers was well positioned in 1928 to take over Herb Wiedoeft's leadership at the Trianon, where Meyers worked regularly. He also composed and recorded 78 RPM records for Brunswick, Victor, Columbia, and his own Vic Meyers' Music label. In 1923 he recorded for Brunswick in Los Angeles, "Mean, Mean Mama" and "Shake It and Break It." Between 1928 and 1929 he co-wrote with different partners a number of songs including "Ada," "Isle of Dreams," and "'Neath the Palms." During the same era, he also recorded for Columbia with his Hotel Butler Orchestra "Anchors Aweigh," as a fox trot, and on the flip side, "Bow Down to Washington." In 1932 he left the music world to become Washington State's Lieutenant Governor, a position he held for the next 20 years. He remained active in state government politics serving as Secretary of State for two terms beginning in 1956.

In a 1926 *Musicland* ad, "Vic and The Boys" were advertised as "Not out to set the world afire, just a bunch of young fellows trying to get along." Others, however, such as early African American cruise ship and service worker, Charles Lewis, recall that Meyers knew how to politically fight black club owners on the wrong side of Seattle's unwritten turf wars. Lewis remembered that after Meyers opened his Club Victor at 2221 Fourth Avenue, the bandleader pressured Russell "Noodles" Smith out of his downtown location at the Golden West Hotel on 710 Seventh Avenue and made Noodles move back to the Jackson Street area, where Seattle confined its black entertainment scene.

20.) Vic Meyers Orchestra, circa 1928. Meyers in back row to right of bassist. Kirwin photo courtesy of A.F. of M. Local 76-493.

A relatively bright spot for Local 493 musicians in their proscribed working territory in and around Jackson Street was the club scene, particularly in the quasi-legal speakeasy rooms. Among the most famous of these was the Black and Tan. In the parlance of the day this name meant a place where blacks and whites could mingle without fear. Or in one of Duke Ellington's eloquent phrases, "where people of all races and colors mixed together for the purpose of fulfilling their social aspirations." Seattle's Black and Tan first saw life in 1922 in a basement when Noodles Smith and Blackie Williams, opened a new club on Jackson Street called The Alhambra. Subsequent ads referred to it as the "Colored Waiters, Porters and Cooks Club, Inc." Ten years later various national acts such as Duke Ellington, Cab Calloway, and Louis Armstrong, who worked primarily white venues like the Orpheum Theatre downtown, came by the Black and Tan after their shows. Joining 493 band members onstage were other national acts including Gene Coy and His Black Aces, Eddie Durham and an All-Star Girl Orchestra, and Ernie Fields, "The Crown Prince of Swing." Period photographer Al Smith recalled an aspect of Seattle's "tolerance policy" firsthand and how it affected the club.

"Oh, people came there... all hours of the morning. I remember in the late hours the police would come in there. And I knew the policemen well, 'cause one of 'em and I went to school together... So, he comes in there and he just closes down the whole house (laughs.) So evidently, they had not gotten their cut... That's how the joints, the gambling places and that stayed open. They paid off to stay open. That was a way of life."

The bass drumhead in the photo opposite and the fact that the photographer, Robert Wright, was the Black & Tan co-owner Noodles Smith's nephew, makes probable that this was the Black and Tan house band. Seattle's complex racial relations are on display in the accompanying photo. In addition to the African American clarinet, trombone, and piano players, there is also an Asian American or Filipino American trumpeter, and a female black drummer. The sheet music on the piano is for "Honolulu Cabaret," music by Lew Hays, and Lyrics by Will J. Hart, published by Jerome H. Remick & Co. in 1916.

21.) The Black and Tan Jazz Orchestra, circa 1928. Robert Wright photograph, courtesy Esther Hall Mumford.

By 1926 radio helped popularize this new music called jazz. Seattle mirrored a national pattern with white "legitimate" musicians and orchestras benefiting almost exclusively from this technological breakthrough. A year earlier, white Local 76 met with "management of radio stations" to ensure that their membership got these jobs and Local 493 players did not. A few years later things began to change and in 1931 black jazz musicians could be heard in national broadcasts. A young would-be trumpeter and eventual 493 unionist, Floyd Standifer, fondly recalled hearing these early broadcasts. At the time Standifer lived in Gresham, Oregon. There he tuned in to late night NBC affiliate, WENR remote broadcasts by Earl "Fatha" Hines from the Grand Terrace in Chicago. These made such an impression on the youngster that he vowed there and then to become a jazz musician. Historical evidence is scant for local Emerald City black musicians on radio during the 1920s and 1930s. However, 493's President Gerald Wells played live broadcasts on KOL during the 1920s. In the thirties, New Orleans famed clarinetist and saxophonist, and presumed 493 member, Joe Darensbourg, had his own show on KXA. Also, during the 1930s, Filipino band member Frank Molina of Bremerton recalled doing KJR live broadcasts along the Snohomish Highway in rooms like the Green Mill Roadhouse.

Here's Louis Armstrong front and center in a 1931 photo with the band of Panamanian Luis Russell. This particular jazz performance was broadcast on New Orleans radio station WSMB. Illustrating the depths of racism there, however, a white deejay refused to "announce that nigger man" during the live remote. This despite Armstrong's popularity, acclaim, and earlier triumphs in Chicago and New York. Pops didn't miss a beat though, and had the orchestra hit a chord and announced himself. Six years later Pops got the last laugh. In 1937 he broke the color barrier in radio once and for all, hosting Fleischman Yeast-sponsored national broadcasts.

22.) Louis Armstrong Leading the Luis Russell Big Band at a 1931 "live" New Orleans WSMB radio broadcast. V. Paddio photograph, New Orleans courtesy of the Louis Armstrong House Museum, Accession 1996.39-19.

Enlarged for detail and shown opposite is Powell Barnett's Local 493 delegate badge from the 37th annual American Federation of Musicians' convention. A rare example of Local 493 memorabilia, Barnett's badge confirms his participation at the 1932 Los Angeles event. Making an early pitch for an end to segregated unions, Barnett spoke with "eight or ten Negro convention delegates." But these Jim Crow union officers, who "had access to the gravy... and did not want to give it up" gave Barnett the run around. Never one to be outmaneuvered, the resourceful trade unionist decided to "take the bull by the horns and talk to the executive committee." Unable to push his idea through at the 1932 session, Barnett succeeded in enlisting one Ray Jackson to establish a national office to "discourage dual locals." Jackson became an "Assistant to the President" and held this position until 1940. In this job he worked to "discourage the establishment of dual locals and (to) persuade the musicians to join into one union." Following a national pattern, most major cities from the turn of the century until the 1950s, 1960s, up to the early 1970s, had segregated musicians' unions. Among the exceptions to this rule were the AFM unions of New York, Detroit, and Portland, Oregon.

Yet Barnett was also a political realist. Ten years earlier in 1922 he fought hard for the establishment of a Jim Crow YMCA on East Madison, reasoning that "half a loaf is better than none." This community institution quickly went on to become a focal point for African American youth, a place where blacks could have dances with music provided by members of their own community. For many years, journeyman musicians like Floyd Standifer, Quincy Jones, and Buddy Catlett learned to perform there, first in the swing style and then on to the wilder terrain of bebop jazz.

23.) Powell Barnett's 1932 American Federation of Musicians' Delegate Badge – Los Angeles Convention. Courtesy of Karen Smith Surall.

Here is a rare photograph of drummer and bandleader Gene Coy and his Black Aces rhythm section. Alongside it is a 1938 ad for an appearance by Coy with an 11-piece band at the Black and Tan, then billing itself as a cabaret. A hard-swinging, territory band originally headquartered in Amarillo, Texas, Coy's Aces featured some of the Southwest's most influential musicians. These included his wife Andrus or Ann, who "played piano like a man," Carl "Tatti" Smith, Alton Moore, Budd Johnson, and Tyree Johnson. Ben Webster was with Coy for nine months from 1929 to 1930 and may have played an Ace's Seattle show during this time. Coy was known for a rollicking, "rambunctious, two-beat style" and toured constantly beginning in 1927. Playing Denver at that time as the Happy Black Aces, Coy so influenced Denver bandleader George Morrison that Morrison promptly made big changes in his more established orchestra. In 1929 as a Seattle resident, Coy no doubt impressed the locals when his little big band played the Butler Hotel, as earlier noted, normally a white musicians only venue. The record indicates that Coy also played Washington Hall in 1933, and thereafter throughout the decade, using Seattle as home base. In addition to West Coast work, Coy's peripatetic band worked a circuit throughout Canada, the Midwest, the East Coast, and Mexico. From 1938 to 1941 Coy featured guitarist and bassist Alvin "Junior" Raglin, who went on to fame with Duke Ellington from 1941 – 1945. When Raglin was in Seattle during the late 1930's, he profoundly impressed Seattle Local 76 stalwart and inveterate jam session member Al Turay. Raglin, albeit misnamed as "Alvin Rankin" can be found with Coy and a 13-piece version of the Aces playing in wide-open Grand Coulee, Washington in January 1939, when the band is listed as "all 493" musicians. Drummer Coy also featured eventual tenor saxophonist star and Seattle resident, Dick Wilson. In 1933 Wilson played with Coy's Aces in a band which included Los Angeles brothers Clyde and Allen Durham, Tatti Smith, and McClure "Red Mack" Morris on tuba, trombone, and trumpet, along with Gene and Ann. Bebop trumpet ace, Howard McGhee, recalled Depression time travels with Coy, where the hard-pressed leader, "didn't pay nobody. We go play, and play and play, and he wind up probably giving you two dollars. I said, 'Jiminy, this ain't it!" During 1935 – 1937 John "Streamline" Ewing and trumpeter Douglas "Slits" Byars confirmed tough times with The Aces as well, eventually departing the Emerald City for Los Angeles – broke and "like the hobos in the box cars."

During the 1930's jazz seems to have taken hold locally, particularly with Seattle's society population at smaller venues such as the Black and Tan. Robert Wright, black nightclub owner and entrepreneur Russell "Noodles" Smith's nephew reminisced, "In 1935 and 1936 you could see as many white people on 12th and Jackson at midnight as you'd see on Third and Union at mid-day." (The Black and Tan was located at 12th and Jackson.)

24.) Gene Coy and His Happy Black Aces rhythm section, Seattle, circa 1938-1941. L-R: Clyde Durham, tuba; Andrus (Ann) Coy, piano; Gene Coy, drums/leader; Alvin "Junior" Raglin, bass. Photo courtesy Peter Vacher. **Gene Coy and His 11 Black Aces play the Black and Tan at 12th and Jackson, November 20, 1938.** Ad from the *Northwest Independent*. Courtesy University of Washington Libraries microfilm collection.

Shown opposite, the Manila Tropical Troubadours are an example of a "gray area" regarding Seattle's black and white union membership. The Troubadours were a group of Filipino jazz and pop musicians who from 1933-1940 worked the Rizal Club. This venue was named for the Filipino revolutionary, author, and physician Jose Rizal, and was a local Filipino gathering place and favorite for jazz musicians. (Located above the Tokiwa Hotel at Jackson near Maynard in the International District, the colorful room was also immortalized in Carlos Bulosan's 1943 novel, *America Is In The Heart*). The Manila Tropical Troubadours, a.k.a. The Moonlight Serenaders were the house band at the Rizal. As such it seems logical for them to have been union musicians. But according to Frank Osias they were never asked to join either the predominantly black Musicians' Local 493 or white Local 76. In a case of Jim Crow meets the Invisible Man, Osias's band was never pressured to join either union, yet another wrinkle in the two unions' complex territory and membership rules.

Osias played taxi dances at the club. This arrangement had men pay ten cents per dance with "the girls." According to the alto saxophonist, the band played "waltzes, fox trots, blues for jitterbugging, and a little bit of jazz," along with rumbas, cha cha's, and Spanish-inflected music. Songs included: "Getting Sentimental," "I'm Confessin'," "I'll Get By," "Blue Skies," "Lazy River," "Tuxedo Junction," and the getting-hot vehicle, "That Naughty Waltz" pictured.

25.) That Naughty Waltz. lyrics by Edwin Stanley and music by Sol P. Levy. Image courtesy of the Lilly Library, Indiana University, Bloomington, Indiana.

26.) The Manila Troubadours, circa 1933. Left to right: Santiago, trumpet; Ernie Bantinan, trumpet; Epiong Colica, banjo and guitar; Frank Osias, alto sax; Julian Costillo, saxophones; Rosenzo Calica, saxophones; Hervasio Hacildo, violin; and Marcas Sison, drums. Jackson Studio photo courtesy Frank and Don Osias.

This 1933 photograph offers an interior view of the Rizal Social Club. In this shot Frank Osias is seated third from left cradling his alto saxophone in his lap. His wife, who was white and originally from Cave Junction, Oregon, is seated eighth from the right in the front row wearing a man's hat with a glass to her mouth. The two met in Oregon during a tour, and promptly married, which was illegal as miscegenation in California until the late 1940s but not in Washington where they resided.

For his pay, Osias started off receiving $3 a night, which eventually went to "$45 a week and they took care of board and room... Lots of fun, but not much money." Throughout the 1930s these two Filipino bands traveled an extensive Western states circuit playing "Granges, parties, rodeos, and theaters" at Yreka, Eureka, Crescent City in California; Cave Junction, Benton, Grants Pass, and Roseburg in Oregon; and Yakima, Sunnyside, Wenatchee in Washington, and as far away as Salt Lake City, Utah for a 1937 tour. Unlike their black or white counterparts, the band never seems to have paid union travel dues at such performances.

27.) The Moonlight Serenaders at the Rizal Social Club perform for a costume party on May 14, 1933. Jackson Studio photograph courtesy of Frank and Don Osias.

A red-letter day for Seattle came on May 17, 1934, when Duke Ellington's Orchestra first came to town in two Pullman railway cars. A front page story appeared in Seattle's African American newspaper, The Northwest Enterprise. It noted that Ellington's "original orchestra" had recently performed in England for the Prince of Wales. (Attending an Ellington 1933 London concert was the 14 year old son of the Turkish ambassador to London, Nesuhi Ertegan, who would go on to fortune and fame in the jazz world, later founding Atlantic Records with his brother Ahmet.) The article provides a glimpse into some of the excitement fans and certainly Seattle's black Local 493 musicians' union members must have felt. Ellington's band arrived in style and did not have to suffer as many of the slings and arrows of discrimination on their overnight adventures as other bands did. Duke's manager, Irving Mills, got around hotel and restaurant segregation by chartering two Pullman railway cars plus a "seventy-foot baggage car" for the band. Emblazoned with DUKE ELLINGTON on the cars' sides, the trains were positioned at tour city's rail stations where automobiles met them. Featured performers at the time included vocalist Ivie Anderson, and dancer, Earl "Snakehips" Tucker in a program of "song, dance, and comedy..."

Increased tour activity by such national bands helped Local 493 musicians directly in at least three ways, in addition to the very real benefits associated with "name" acts popularizing and making acceptable the new art form in Seattle. First, when touring bands came to town, they paid work dues directly to the segregated local. Second, 493 members sometimes directly benefited when national bands needed musicians who had dropped out of tours and so substituted local players. Third, the American Federation of Musicians' policy of "featherbedding," allowed Local 493's Business Agent to place extra musicians on the payroll when a given venue like the Trianon required more players than were on tour. However, all of this was complicated, particularly when it came to transfer dues payment. For example, Local 493 did receive transfer dues from Los Angeles' black Local 767 in 1935 for an appearance by the Les Hite orchestra at the Olympic Hotel. Then in 1937 eleven members of the largest black musicians' union, Chicago Local 208, also paid travelling dues to 493. The Chicago union musicians were part of the Noble Sissle and Eubie Blake vaudeville revue, *Shuffle Along,* whose bandleader was a then unknown pianist, named Nat ("King") Cole, along with the legendary trombonist, John L. Thomas. However, in 1936 and 1938, L.A.'s Local 767 forced band leaders Lionel Hampton and Les Hite to pay their traveling dues for Seattle shows to white Local 76. Further muddying the waters in April 1937, New York City's Local 802 (never segregated) had its members including Duke Ellington's band pay their traveling dues also to the white Local 76.

28.) "Meet The Duke," Ellington Orchestra's first Seattle performance
May 17, 1934 at John Hamrick's Music Hall. *Northwest Enterprise* clip
courtesy University Library System, University of Washington.

The following year on August 15, 1935, Lionel Hampton played his first Seattle show at the New Rex Theatre. This was also his first tour as a band leader, where he was billed as "Champion Drum Beater" prior to his "King of the Vibes" role. On this first tour, Hamp's tough-as-nails business partner and wife, Gladys, hired a British booking agent named Jack Hamilton, who absconded with most of the band's advance deposits. The ten-piece band travelled in Gladys's 1929 Dodge and another 1927 Ford. Struggling against fiercely segregated conditions on the West Coast, Hamp's men could not obtain rooms in hotels and were forced to stay in black boarding houses, private homes, or sleep in their cars. "Whites Only" restaurants forced them to patronize grocery stores and the occasional Chinese restaurant. At times they were so broke that their meals consisted of rice with catsup. On the same tour, in then virulently racist Portland, Oregon, the bandleader was refused service at a lowly hot dog stand, despite being a "standing room only" hit at that city's McEnroy Ballroom.

Following their New Rex Theatre Seattle performance, Hamp's band quit en masse to join a cruise ship. However, the resourceful Gladys turned the tables on the indignities of the road and a crooked agent. Back home, she described the tour as a big success to Frank Sebastian, the owner of the luxurious New Cotton Club in Los Angeles. After this each night Sebastian introduced the Hampton band as just back from a "triumphant West Coast Tour."

29.) First Seattle Performance of "Champion Drum Beater" Lionel Hampton, August 15, 1935.
Northwest Enterprise front page clipping courtesy University Library System, University of Washington.

At the end of 1935, Cab Calloway and his New York Orchestra and Cotton Club Revue of thirty five people made their first Seattle appearance at the Paramount. Billed as "His Royal Highness of Hi-De-Ho," Cab was also managed by Irving Mills at this time, who played up Cab's connection with the Harlem Renaissance whites-only nightspot, the Cotton Club. Calloway, originally from Rochester, New York, began his music career in Chicago where he was studying pre-law at Crane College. After singing with Louis Armstrong, and Marian Hardy and his Alabamians in Chicago, Cab took over this band and headed east with it in 1928. Calloway recorded with the Alabamians in 1929 for Victor. Then, at the behest of manager Mills, the maestro became the new leader of Andy Preer's band, the Missourians. This band became Cab's and followed Duke Ellington's "Jungle Orchestra" into the gangster-run Cotton Club in early 1931, where they quickly became a sensation. Later that same year, Calloway and band suffered through a Mills-booked tour of the deep South. There the maestro received racist treatment replete with calls from a white audience for Cab's lynching at a Virginia Beach performance when the band bus broke down. To Mills credit, he had also booked Calloway (and Duke Ellington) on successful European tours in 1932.

As mentioned, when name musicians' union bands such as Fletcher Henderson and Cab hit town real economic benefits came to Seattle's black Musicians' Union Local 493. Those benefits also spilled over in other ways for Seattle's African American community. For example, the big band musicians always made it a point to hit clubs such as the Black and Tan and other places when in Seattle for camaraderie and jams (where they worked with 493 members.) In addition, band members stayed at black hotels such as Noodles Smith's Golden West Hotel.

Seattle had its own Cotton Club, located "on the Seattle-Tacoma Highway, near the Meadows on Marginal Way," where members of Seattle's Local 493 regularly performed. Indeed, as early as 1931, (Earl) "Whaley's Cotton Pickers Orchestra" were featured regularly at the local venue.

30.) The Cab Calloway Orchestra plays Seattle December 15, 1935. *Northwest Enterprise* front page clipping courtesy University Library System, University of Washington.

Local 493 member and bandleader, Earl Whaley, is depicted here high above the Shanghai skyline in 1937. Whaley took a septet to the St. Anna Ballroom, at 80 Love Lane, in the wide-open International District of Shanghai, China in July 1934. The original band featured Whaley on tenor and alto saxophones, with other Seattle players Palmer Johnson on piano, Wayne Adams on baritone sax, Earl West on guitar, Oscar Hurst on trumpet, Fate Williams trombone, and Gilbert "Punkin" Austin at the trap drums.

Beginning as early as 1922, Shanghai provided well-paid work for black musicians, who were treated with respect and dignity by their hosts. In a letter home, Palmer Johnson wrote that their band was a "big hit" and that Shanghai was a truly "cosmopolitan city with representatives of every race in the population," marred only by the "most rude-mannered and impolite of all races... the American white man." Johnson is not in this shot, having departed earlier in 1937. Featured in this nonette is the Shanghai-based pianist Pomping Villa. Personnel also changed for trombone, trumpet, tenor, and bass. The latter instrument was played by Reginald Jones, who joined Whaley after working with trumpeter Buck Clayton's Shanghai band. Known as "Jonesy," the bassist was another veteran from Gene Coy's Aces who'd settled in Seattle during this period. Note too that the photo is signed "Jonesy."

Other Seattle musicians including 493 member and bandleader Jimmy Adams, as well as Nisei vocalist and Japanese Columbia Records artist, Chizuko Miyagawa, (a.k.a. Harumi Miyagawa), were in Shanghai at this same time. Adding spice to the Shanghai mix were prominent musicians such as Chicago-based pianist and Erskine Tate sideman, Teddy Weatherford, along with Buck Clayton. Clayton led his 14-piece "Harlem Gentlemen of Jazz" from 1934-1936 at a Chinese-owned club and casino called the Canidrome. Expatriate White Russian jazz musicians like Oleg and Igor Lundstrem also worked at Shanghai's Paramount ballroom. All in all, there was plenty of hot jazz in the "City of Blazing Light" for Whaley, Palmer Johnson, and company. With decent period wages of $50 to $200 weekly, the crew had money enough for a good time, in "Yellow Babylon." Guidebooks speculated "Joy, gin and jazz. There's nothing puritanical about Shanghai." Something of an understatement, given that sex and drugs including heroin could all be had from hotel room service.

31.) Earl Whaley's Orchestra – Shanghai 1937. L-R: Pomping Villa, piano; Reginald Jones, bass and tuba; Ernest Clark, trombone; Calvin Temple, trumpet; Earl Whaley saxes, leader; Wayne Adams, alto sax; Henry Allen, tenor sax; Earl West, guitar; and Gilbert "Punkin" Austin, drums and violin. Photo courtesy Frank Driggs.

Just back from China, Palmer Johnson next held forth at one of Seattle's most desirable clubs, the 411. Johnson was a 493 man "with the class of Billy Kyle," and was one of the locals who was a first call jazz performer, someone who "could work with anybody's band." Born in 1907 in Houston, Texas, Johnson was raised near Los Angeles's famed Central Avenue. He began playing violin at seven, but eventually took up the piano. At seventeen he was playing professionally in the various clubs of Central Avenue. Four years later in 1928, he moved to Seattle where his first job was at Lake City Way's Maryland Tavern. Known as a "fixture of the late night set," Palmer and his trio worked extensively during Prohibition times at the China Castle, which became the Jolly Roger. A gifted entertainer, he was also popular with "other musicians in town (who) were going to school on him, as it were." In this 1938 ad, the 6th Avenue South club, half a block off Jackson Street, is also advertising an illegal, according to AFM strictures, "Jam Session." During the late 1930s the 411 was the place for name players to drop in as well, and Duke Ellington, Ben Webster, and Louis Armstrong all came by when in town.

Seattle guitarist, bassist, Local 76er and Local 493 fellow traveler, Al Turay, who'd earlier made the switch from playing "cowboy guitar" to jazz, fondly recalled the 411 during this era,

> "...They'd get going after midnight. They were after hours places, illegal, but that's where the action was. I used to go down to hear a piano player - Palmer Johnson. He was the head man around there... That was the general situation. You'd finish your gig and then go down there. If you could play at all they'd let you sit in. So, a lot of your ballads, you accumulated based on your forays into that scene."

32.) Bar-B-Que at the 411 Club with Palmer Johnson, 1938. Ad from *Northwest Enterprise* November 18, 1938. Courtesy University of Washington Libraries.

Ashades-visaged Dick Wilson wails on tenor sax with Andy Kirk's "Clouds of Joy" at a 1941 Seattle performance. Sadly, this was only months before an untimely death at 30 on November 24th, 1941. He was an Emerald City resident from 1916 until the mid-1920s when he moved to Los Angeles. In 1928 Wilson returned to Seattle when he was 17 and began studying with Joe Darensbourg, who got him a job with Portland big band leader Don Anderson in 1929. Darensbourg also lent Wilson his "old Holton" tenor saxophone, allowing Wilson to go professional with Anderson. Wilson went on to work for a year at this, his first job as a tenor man. Back in Seattle he returned the Holton, having purchased his own tenor, and played for a "month or two" with Darensbourg locally at the Jungle Temple in a band with 493 man Jimmy Adams on trumpet, Baby Borders on drums, and Babe Hackley on piano. Next, Wilson went out on a West Coast tour with Gene Coy and his Black Aces. Following studies with Franz Roth in Denver and a spell playing in Zack Whyte's Band there, Wilson joined the Andy Kirk Orchestra in 1936. With the Clouds of Joy until the end, his highly original tenor sax stylings formed a perfect counterfoil for the music of fellow band member, pianist, composer, and arranger Mary Lou Williams. An influential soloist and performer, Wilson was a gifted improviser, "very advanced" with his own style and sound.

33.) Tenor Sax Ace, Dick Wilson soloing with the Andy Kirk Band in 1941 at Seattle's Senator's Ballroom. Al Smith photo.

The sharply clad lads opposite were all members of Billy Tolles' Men of Jazz, later known as The Savoy Boys. (Check the prominent BT on the music stands.) Most all the band members were Garfield High School students at the time of this early 1940s photograph. Leader Tolles received musical training in the Mount Zion Baptist Church Junior Choir and was prominent later in the Seattle jazz scene and a card-carrying Local 493 Musicians' Union member. At Garfield, Tolles started off on trumpet, playing in the marching band. Along with school mates Gerald Brashear and Sonny Booker, he also played in a swing band of Charlie Blackwell's called the Four Sharps.

This photograph was taken at the Trianon rather than the Savoy Hall, the latter room where these high school musicians came to fame (and the inspiration for their name.) The Savoy was located at 21st Avenue and East Madison Street and was leased by local pool hall owner Lem Honeysuckle who renamed the former Anzier Theater after the famous Harlem jazz nightclub. A front page *Northwest Enterprise* story, replete with banner headlines and Tolles photo with his tenor sax, cites the "Grand Opening of The Savoy" on Saturday night, March 13, 1943. "Billie (sic) Tolles and his gang of musical cats" were billed that night as "the official blues chasers for the Savoy." After their run, this big band was replaced by another young Seattle black ensemble, the Frank Roberts Four.

In addition to Tolles, other musicians depicted who went on to varying degrees of fame included the Brashear brothers, Sonny Booker, and Major Pigford, who later worked in the Al Pierre Orchestra and the Bumps Blackwell Junior Band. Pigford recalled that with the Savoy Boys,

> *"...We played a lot of things from written music, from orchestrations I guess that Billy bought. Then a lot of things we just put together by head. We featured Bobby Catlett on "Floyd's Guitar Blues." Sonny Booker could play the heck out of "Stardust." Buddy Brashear played "After Hours." We also did "Tuxedo Junction," "Stompin' at the Savoy," and "Blues in the Night."*

34.) Billy Tolles' Men of Jazz, later known as The Savoy Boys, circa 1941. Back row: trumpets, Don Alexander, Sonny Booker, Carl Valley. Middle row: Buddy Brashear, piano; Delbert Brown, drums; Bobby Catlett, guitar and bass; Richard Yarbrough and Major Pigford, trombones. Front Row: standing, unknown. Saxophones: Floyd Franklin, George Francis, Billy Tolles, and Gerald Brashear. Al Smith photo courtesy Black Heritage Society of Washington State, Inc.

Band leader, pianist, club owner and Local 493 Musicians' Union regular, Al Pierre is shown here with his group. Of those pictured, drummer Vernon Brown and bassist Bob Marshall remained active within the union until amalgamation. Unlike larger white musicians' unions, Local 493 members were not solely administrators and worked as both musicians and union officials or volunteers. Al Pierre was originally from Tacoma, where his pioneering grandparents had moved to avoid slavery. Pierre left the City of Destiny in the mid-20s to work in the greener pastures of Los Angeles, where he gained a reputation as a skilled piano man and sight reader. With such chops, he then moved to Portland in the 1930s, where he worked steadily in rooms ranging from Frat Hall and a speakeasy downtown owned by racketeer Swede Ferguson, to Blue Lake Park and the Dude Ranch, all while holding down a 12 year-stint at Berg's Chalet. Of his time playing in Pierre's band, Clarence "Prince of the Blues" Williams fondly remembered,

> *"He was such a class act and an excellent piano player. Not modern, but very, very good. He was the leader of us all. He taught me how to be a working musician, how to be professional, being on time and properly dressed. Something your normal music teacher never gets around to telling you... I couldn't even read whole notes before I met Al. He showed me the five finger approach to reading music and it changed my whole approach to playing the blues. Ask anyone alive about Al Pierre. They'll tell you."*

Pierre remained equally busy for the next two decades in Seattle. One of his band members, tenor saxophonist Ulysses "Jabo" Ward, recalled playing in one of Pierre's bands at the Union club from 1943-1950. Ward played "four hours a night," coming on as the second band at 1:00 a.m. and working five and six nights a week. He made "$70 a week," but with the "kitty" and other tips usually netted an additional $10 a night for "over $100 a week. Good money for those days." Beverly Kelly, Al Pierre's niece, Garfield High School alum, and life-long Seattle arts fan explained that the enterprising Pierre also ran Al's Lucky Hour Tavern on Yesler and funded a baseball club during this time. *(See pages 70-71)* "... Everybody adored Al. They really did," she recalled.

35.) The Al Pierre Band, c. 1945. Left to right Leon Vaughan – trumpet, Vernon Brown – drums, William Joseph – alto saxophone, Al Hickey – tenor saxophone, Bob Marshall – bass, Al Pierre – piano. Al Smith photo.

Shown bartending at the black Elks Club in 1942, Dorothy Lomax relaxes with a cigarette. The Club was located at 662 Jackson and featured live music. Ray Charles played his first professional engagement there. Later, Seattle pianist and band leader Cecil Young gigged there for close to a year. The two soldiers are unidentified, but according to Lomax never returned from their wartime activities. Moving to Seattle from Denver in 1939, Lomax worked several years as a waitress downtown, first for a "Chinese fellow" where she helped break the color barrier. She next "did a little bit of dancing and singing," owning an "associate or temporary" card from Local 493 but did not formally join the union because she never made a career as a full time singer.

As a bartender and waitress, she earned a living at various rooms in and around downtown and Jackson Street. In a glimpse into a trusting world now long gone, Lomax recalled,

> *"I'd be at a club and I'd sit there with a bankroll and open it up and pay for my drinks. People used to leave their money on the bar. You'd go to some place and if you were with a trusted bartender, people would go to another place and just leave their money there. And when they came back, I'd take maybe a dollar out of it for (safe) keeping and say, 'Hey. Here's your money.' I had so much money behind the bar sometimes I wouldn't know whose money belonged to who."*

36.) Dorothy Lomax behind the black Elks Club bar with soldiers, circa 1942. Photo courtesy of Dorothy Lomax.

Two photographs spotlight black Seattle baseball teams in the late 1940s. Above right is Powell Barnett's Royal Colored Giants. Below is Al Pierre with the Carver Athletic Club. Segregated black baseball was popular in Seattle from 1911 to 1951. It is no accident that two important Local 493 musicians were active in the favorite pastime. Beginning in 1923 club owner Doc Hamilton sponsored a black baseball team and a Sunday afternoon tradition at Garfield Park became a destination for Seattle African Americans. Powell Barnett was the founder and manager of the Royal Colored Giants. He also helped organize other umpires and built community support for the teams. Recalling these days, Beverly Kelly recalled, "Al (Pierre) was instrumental in funding a baseball team. He paid for the uniforms, the bats, and balls... Here's a picture of Powell Barnett in the suit. He was an umpire and was active in the union."

The connection between jazz and baseball is not isolated to Seattle and had a long tradition. In the 1930s other jazz greats like Cab Calloway, Louis Armstrong, Count Basie, Benny Goodman, and Harry James (a baseball fanatic) among others all had their own teams in the "Big Band League." Indeed, there is an account of a baseball battle of the bands with unlikely hitter, Lester Young knocking an "inside the park home run" during a game between the Basie and Goodman big bands. (Goodman won.) During this same time in 1936, a young high school graduate named Nathaniel Coles had to choose between a career in baseball, coming to the attention of two Negro League scouts, or music. The latter prevailed and Nat "King" Cole became famous first as a jazz pianist and then as a popular singer.

37.) Powell Barnett in vest and tie, along with Art Harris third row in cap and Billy Tolles in wool stocking cap, Henry Twaites next to Tolles on right, and Richard Dean, face partially obscured behind Twaites, all of the Royal Colored Giants, circa late 1940s.

38.) Al Pierre with the Carver Athletic Club, 1949. Back row left to right Bennet Wilborn, Dewey Tate, Henry Twaites, Brennan King, Cal Hubbard, Al McKenzie, Cleto Barnes, and Richard Dean. Front row Chris Tull, Collins, Currie, Jack Alexander, Al Pierre, Doc Wayman, David Dinish, Don Lee Moore, and Bob Flowers. *Both photos courtesy of Douglas Q. Barnett.*

This interior photograph showcases a mid-1940s social event at the venerable 908 Club, then run by Dick Ruffin and Nixie Smith. In its heyday in the 1920s under John H. "Doc" Hamilton's direction, his Barbecue Pit, located at 908 12th Avenue, was a prohibition-era speakeasy. There Seattle's elite, or those just out for a good time, could hear jazz, imbibe their favorite illegal beverage, and gamble. Society man and author Henry Broderick, eloquently, albeit with period racism, put it this way,

> *"Doc was easily the best-known nightspot proprietor in the city's history. A tall good-looking darkey, his features fairly exude affability. An extra-ordinary conversationalist, he never presumed upon acquaintance or friendship... Doc Hamilton was a Negro deluxe... He created atmospheric night life with a flavor all its own..."*

Multi-reeds man and pioneer of early jazz and syncopated sound Joe Darensbourg played this room, or "joint" in his parlance. In 1928 along with 493 unionists, Palmer Johnson on piano, guitarist Bill Page, and drummer Gilbert "Punkin" Austin, Darensbourg played Hamilton's establishment. A student of New Orleans music patriarch, Alphonse Picou, Darensbourg related that local pianist Oscar Holden and drummer Bill Hoy also worked there.

Shown here are Local 493 President and Caribbean-born impresario, flautist and tenor man, Gerald and Elizabeth Dean Wells in the first booth. In the next booth are Harry Walker, Josie Hall, Marvie Williamson, and Frank Fair with a waiter. In the next booth is Melvina Squires, and in the last booth is Charlie Russell.

39.) The Engagement of Gertrude Jackson and Nesbit Frazier at the 908 Club, circa mid-1940s. Photo courtesy of Black Heritage Society of Washington, Inc.

This 1944 Seattle map spotlights a sampling of club and hall locations which Local 493 members worked. In addition, it also provides a visual for some of the residences of The Blue Note, Seattle's AFM Local 493 headquarters and informal clubhouse. Initial meetings for Local 493 began in December of 1924 and probably took place at white Local 76's headquarters on 2025 Fourth Avenue and other locations. From the late 1930s through the mid-1940s, Local 493's office was at the homes of Gerald and Elizabeth Dean Wells, first at 401-409 19th Avenue East, and then at 214 20th Street North. From 1948-1949 the Local was headquartered at 1037 Jackson Street, when it was listed as the Musicians' Protective Union. In 1951 its address is given as 418-A Second Avenue. Finally, from 1953 until amalgamation with Local 76 in December 1956, Local 493's location was at a small clubhouse-like building at 1319 East Jefferson Street. This was the locale which Seattle's black musicians fondly referred to as "The Blue Note." In addition to all the normal functions of the union, legendary jam sessions also took place there.

Details remain sketchy as to where Local 493's predecessor, the first black Musicians' Union, Local 458, held its meetings from 1918 through 1924. Thanks to negotiations by Powell Barnett, Charles Adams, and others, the union had access to meeting rooms at the white local on Fourth Avenue, and probably conducted at least some of their business there. Other meeting locations could not be found, and in fact Local 458 did not meet regularly during its last two years.

Of the 1930s days in the Benjamin McAdoo designed four-plex at 401-409 19th Avenue East, Elizabeth Wells recalled,

> *"The Musicians' Union was in our home, in our hallway really. You'd have to pay each year for the charter, and of course, none of them had any money, including my husband. And so, I'd have to get the charter for them. Women were able to find jobs more readily than men."*

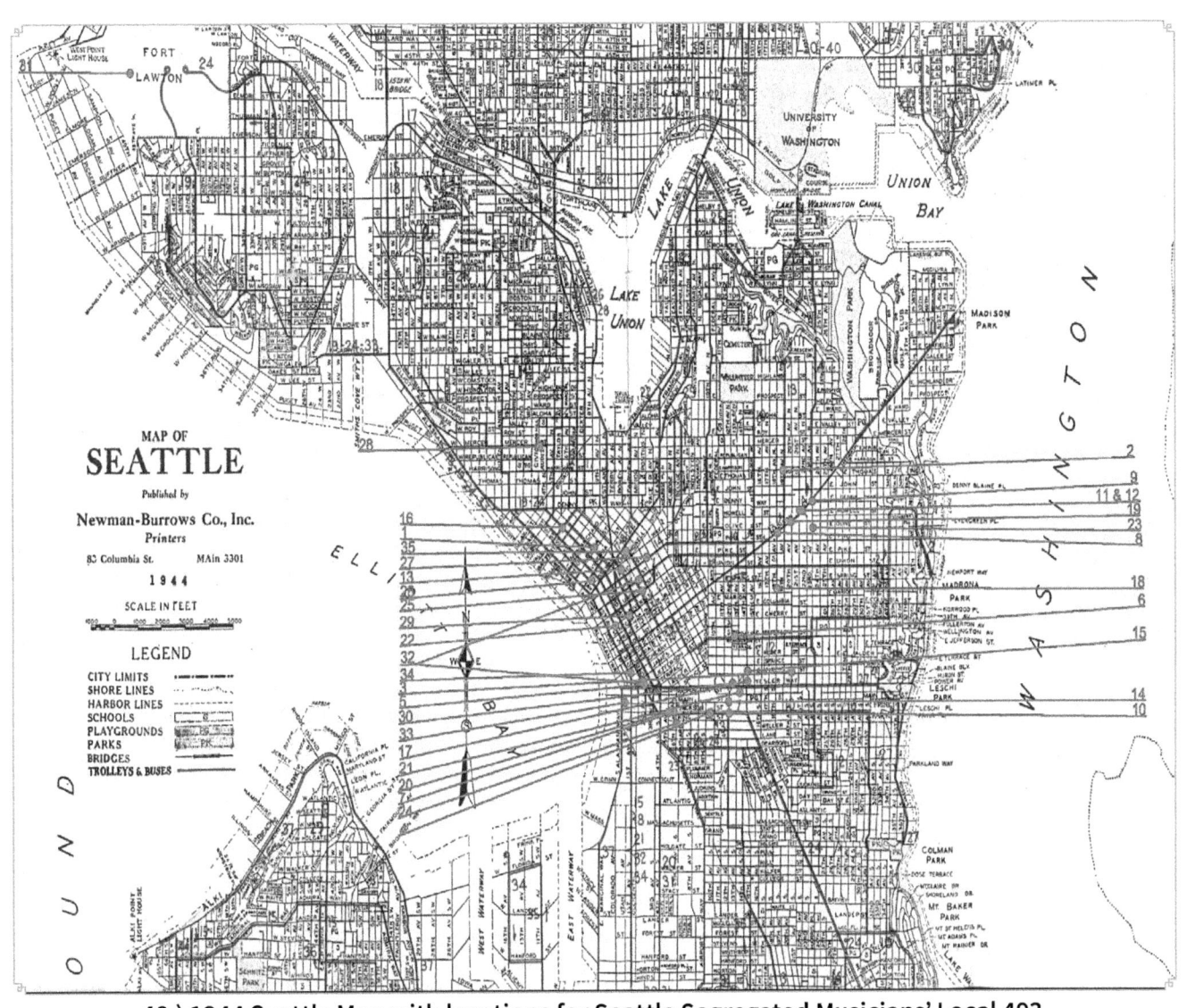

40.) 1944 Seattle Map with locations for Seattle Segregated Musicians' Local 493, Territory Clubs and Halls. Author's collection.

Local 458 & 493 Union Locations

1.) Among the first locations for Local 458 meetings may have been AFM Local 76 headquarters at 2025 Fourth Avenue. The "Colored Musicians' Union" had access to this office from at least 1919. The Labor Temple is also mentioned in 1918.

2.) Local 493 headquartered at 401-409 19th Avenue East, circa late 1930s through early 1940s in the home of Gerald and Elizabeth Dean Wells.

3.) Local 493 at 214 20th Avenue North at Wells' home in 1941.

4.) 1037 Jackson Street when Local 493 is known at the Musicians' Protective Union in 1948 – 1949.

5.) 418-A Second Avenue as Musicians' Protective Union in 1951.

6.) 1319 E. Jefferson Street where the club house Musicians' Union Local 493 is known as "The Blue Note" from 1953-1956.

Select Clubs & Halls:

7.) The Rizal Club, 651-661 Jackson Street second floor.

8.) The Black Elks Club, southeast corner of 18th and Madison.

9.) Washington Social and Educational Club, corner of 23rd and East Madison.

10.) The Black & Tan – Colored Waiters', Porters', and Cooks' Club 404 ½ 12th Avenue South.

11.) Savoy Dance Hall, 22nd Avenue and East Madison Street.

12.) Birdland, 22nd Avenue and East Madison Street.

13.) Nanking Café, 1616 ½ Fourth Avenue, between Pine and Olive Streets.

14.) The Entertainer's Club/ Sessions Playhouse, 12th Avenue South and Main Street.

15.) Washington Hall, 14th Avenue and East Fir Street.

16.) The Trianon, Third Avenue and Wall Street.

17.) The Rocking Chair, 14th Avenue off Yesler Street.

18.) 908 Club, a.k.a. Doc Hamilton's, 908 12th Avenue.

19.) The Mardi Gras, 2045 East Madison Street.

20.) The Ebony Café, Fifth and Jackson Street.

21.) Finnish Hall, Washington Street and 13th Avenue.

22.) The Palomar, Third Avenue and University Street.

23.) The Colored YMCA, 23rd Avenue and Olive Street.

24.) 411 Club, 411 Sixth Avenue South.

25.) Senator's Ballroom, Seventh Avenue and Union Street.

26.) The Moore Theatre, 1932 Second Avenue.

27.) The Paramount Theater, 911 Pine Street.

28.) Seattle Civic Auditorium, Third Avenue North and Mercer.

29.) The Metropolitan Theatre, 415 University Street.

30.) Al's Lucky Hour, 12th Avenue and Yesler Street.

31.) Fort Lawton, as shown.

32.) Shanghai Restaurants, 711 Pike Street, and 100 Second Avenue near Yesler.

33.) Pete's Poop Deck, 77 Main Street.

34.) The Penthouse, First Avenue and Cherry Street.

35.) The Door, 1818 Seventh Avenue.

Local 493 President Gerald Wells, who came from Grenada, Trinidad, or Jamaica depending on the source, was a popular flutist, tenor sax man, and bandleader. He first appears on the West Coast around 1915 playing flute with Sid LeProtti's So Different Jazz Band in San Francisco and Oakland. From there he worked in Honolulu, Los Angeles, and Nogales, New Mexico before coming to Seattle at the end of World War I.

After Powell Barnett, Wells is the dominant personality in guiding Seattle's black musicians' union for many years. Particularly during the 1940s, 493's President Wells debated white union officials over questions of union territory, welcomed AFM union delegates to Seattle at the 46th Annual Convention June 9-14, 1941 with separate segregated performances, and produced numerous shows with local and national talent.

No stranger to controversy, Wells was also taken to task then for presenting a performance labeled "Duke Ellington and Jim Crow" at the Show Box, on First Avenue and Pike Street as advertised March 29, 1940. Following heated editorials and further negotiations, Wells seems to have saved face with a compromise of an additional performance. In what the *Northwest Enterprise* billed as "A Scoop!!" Duke Ellington and Orchestra along with 75 musicians including Gene Coy, Gay Jones, Palmer Johnson et al performed a benefit "First Annual Ball" on April 8, 1940 for Musicians' Local 493 at Finnish Hall. The admission charge was sixty cents.

41.) Long time Local 493 President Gerald Wells, on tenor saxophone center; with Joe Gauff, alto sax; unknown, trumpet; Eddie Davis, drums; Leonard Brooks on piano, possibly Charles Gray, bass. At Todd's circa 1943-44. Photo courtesy Ralph Davis.

The 1940s and particularly the World War II years from 1941-1946 presented a tremendous payday for Local 493 members as Seattle transitioned to a full-blown wartime economy. Fleet-fingered, tenor saxophonist and Local 493 member Jabo Ward fondly recalled those round-the-clock and boomtown days,

> *"Everybody had money. Had Rosie the Riveter out at Boeing. And those guys workin' out at the shipyards had three shifts, see? Three eight hour shifts. People coming and going. It was hustle and bustle. Right here in Seattle."*

All the work brought increased diversity into the Emerald City. Not everyone was happy with some of the changes to the hitherto tightly proscribed worlds of Seattle's black and white populations as the patriarchal figure in this period cartoon makes clear.

42.) "Slum Boulevard and Any Street," March 22, 1944, in *Northwest Enterprise.*
Courtesy University Library System, University of Washington.

Reality mirrors art in a Jackson Street photograph further documenting the changing demographics and social customs of Seattle's black population. This circa 1943-1944 shot finds African American workers drinking and cutting up at 514-518 Jackson Street. Although dress and demeanor are not identical to the previous editorial cartoon, the cigarettes and clowning appear to be the sort of "field" activity which shocked the cartoon stereotypes previously depicted.

Businesses left to right are the Evergreen Tavern, Natco's Bargain House, and the Paramount Café. In 1942 the Evergreen was also known as the Taniguchi Masaru Beer Parlor, and the Paramount Café's listed owner was a Mrs. Yukiko Yoshijima. This ownership points up the interrelations of Seattle's African American and Japanese American communities. However, in 1942 Seattle's Japanese American residents were evacuated from Seattle by the Federal government and placed into various camps throughout the West. A close look at the photograph reveals a Bargain House window sign advertising World War II related shipping to "Europe and Asia." Note also that the Evergreen's "Bottles to Take Out," pitch seems to be working, while a partially obscured concert poster in its window extols a live music event.

43.) "Hustle and Bustle" On the Street. Ogawa photo circa 1940s.
Courtesy University of Washington Libraries, Special Collections, UW27650.

George James "Buddy" Catlett grew up in Seattle. During the 1940s he recalled the tremendous growth of Seattle's black population from 3,879 to between 10,000 to 15,000, and what this meant for the local music scene. The clarinetist and bassist spent his early years in a relatively pastoral Seattle. His influences as a young man came from records, teachers, and greats such as New Orleans clarinetist and band leader Joe Darensbourg as well as local legend Banjoski Adams. But even with this relatively sophisticated musical upbringing, Catlett was unprepared for the raw intensity of a different type of music, brought by newcomers from the South during the World War II boom years. He recalled,

> *"It made you figure out first-hand what you were tryin' to do. Because I had people move in across the street, who were from Lubbock, Texas. And I heard some real blues. Not Duke Ellington's, Jimmy Lunceford's, or Count Basie's... That's sophisticated.*
>
> *"They brought Delta Blues in from Mississippi and Texas – from the cotton fields where the music really came from. And that changes your attitude about intensity. Before everybody's tryin' to make it acceptable to a white dancing audience or a black bourgeois audience (laughs.) Make things 'light' (laughs.)"*

44.) George James "Buddy" Catlett, 493 member and former Louis Armstrong stalwart. Photo courtesy of Buddy Catlett.

Buddy Groves was a professional guitarist, bass player, and 493 union man active during the late 1930s and 1940s in and around Seattle. For over a year in 1937, he was the bassist with a band led by vocalist and tenor man Tootie Boyd. The group also included drummer Junie Bradford and Banjoski Adams and worked near Bellingham at a popular roadhouse called the Shantytown. Thereafter Buddy Groves seems to have gigged steadily up to and including during Seattle's booming war-time years, eventually joining the Merchant Marine. The Groves brothers moved to Seattle from the mining region around Butte, Montana, according to their niece, Francis Demisse. Ms. Demisse recalled that "Uncle Buddy was in the union and then he had his big band. My mother had a band in Montana and then they came here." Francis's Seattle move was in 1931 and was prompted by a desire to be near her Uncles Buddy and Sirless "Sy" Groves. The latter was the well-known entrepreneur who ran the prominent entertainment venue, the Washington Social and Educational Club.

45.) Guitarist, bassist, and 493 trade union man, Buddy Groves, circa 1940s.
Photo courtesy of Francis Demisse.

Al Hickey is shown here as leader of his popular Jive Bombers combo. The band was modeled after the first Jive Bombers group, which Hickey and Harry "Doc" Wheeler led at the WW II-era Great Lakes Naval Facility located near Chicago. Fellow band member John Willis also performed continually in Seattle during the boom town World War II-period. Willis would remain active in the American Federation of Musicians' Protective Union Local 493 for years and was its Secretary-Treasurer from 1948-1956. He was also assigned to the same Great Lakes Navy big band as Hickey and Wheeler. This was a fabled big band which was originally started by Eleanor Roosevelt, and featured national luminaries from the period including Clark Terry, Willie Smith, Marshall Royal, and a then unknown, Los Angeles alto saxophonist, named William "Buddy" Collette, among others.

Hickey and Willis worked together in a regional military band when they were shipped out to Sand Point Naval Station in Seattle. In this and the previous Great Lakes Navy Big Band they played in the saxophone section alongside William Funderberg. "Fundy," Local 493's Business Agent from 1945-1953, was originally from Birmingham, Alabama and led his own popular territorial band. (See Photograph No. 49.) Bob Braxton is also another confirmed 493 man. The mission of the Sand Point Navy band was to bolster the spirit of war workers building the naval aircraft, F-6. The band toured Washington State's defense factories in this capacity.

46.) The Jive Bombers in uniform, l-r Al Hickey, Bob Braxton, William Funderberg, John Willis, and Andrew Wade, circa 1940s.
Photo courtesy William Funderberg.

As Local 493's Business Agent, William Funderberg affirmed that the 1940s were a good time to be a skilled jazz musician. Work was relatively plentiful, particularly in the Jackson Street and waterfront milieus, which made up the bulk of Local 493 territory. As a stalwart representative of union culture, his duties were to collect dues and to make certain that work dues were paid by visiting out-of-town bands. He saw that musicians received scale payments and did not work for receipts from door admissions or for the kitty. In this capacity "Fundy" explained,

> *"I collected the dues and was the troubleshooter for the people in the clubs. Stop that jam session."*

The saxophonist and bandleader proudly upheld the letter of the anti-jamming A.F. of M. policy, despite the feelings of fellow unionists like Elmer Gill who loathed the ruling. The law came about because the International believed that unscrupulous club owners would promote an evening jam session and only pay scale to the rhythm section members and nothing to the others. Though this hard-line ignored a venerable form of jazz education, Funderberg took his work seriously and told both musicians and club owners that the practice they were having fun with, learning from, and (for club owners) making money on, was illegal and must stop. His position pointed up tensions within Local 493.

One of the few pieces of existent 493 ephemera, the *Price List and Working Rules* book, is shown opposite. Note that the printed address of 1037 Jackson Street has been written over and replaced by 1319 Jefferson, the fabled home of The Blue Note clubhouse local. Prices varied with musicians in "Class C: Taverns" who were required to play "4 hours or Less per day" receiving $48.00. A 493 musician's scale for "Casual or Regular Engagements" was considerably less at $9.00 for the same hourly commitment.

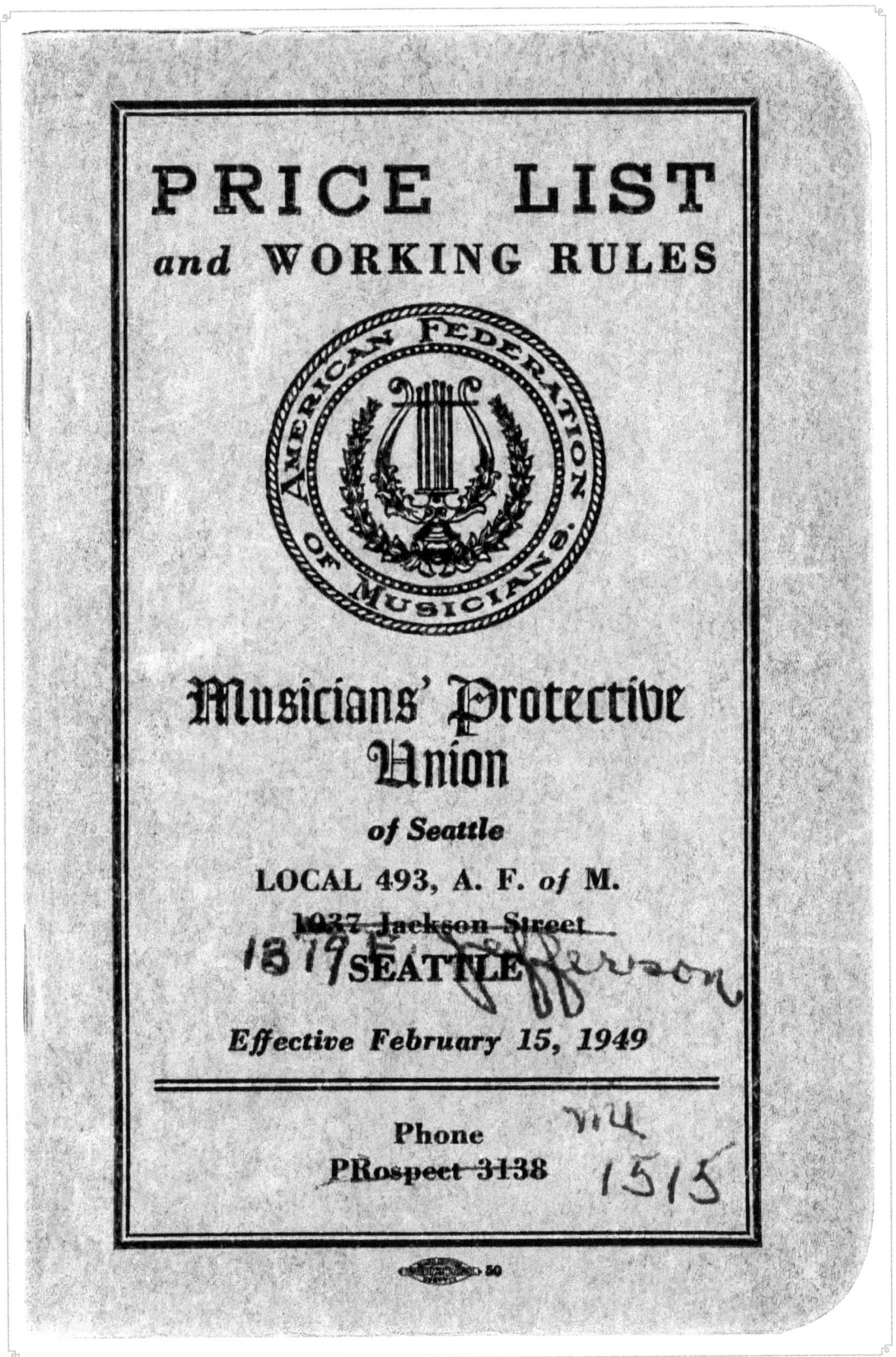

47.) Musicians' Protective Union of Seattle Local 493 Price List, 1949.
Courtesy Local A. F. of M. 76-493.

Pictured playing baritone saxophone, William Funderberg and his big band perform in a Birmingham, Alabama locale around 1940. Funderberg was a product of music patriarch John "Fess" Whatley, who has been labeled "the most stunningly successful music educator in the history of Alabama…" Fellow alums of Whatley's Birmingham Industrial School band included: Erskine Hawkins, Sammy Lowe, Jo Jones, Avery Parrish, and Sonny Blount, a.k.a. Sun Ra.

Growing up under a strictly segregated system, Funderberg was forced to adhere to rigid Jim Crow social strictures. Yet he transcended these boundaries and profited from the discipline and spit-and-polish drive instilled by Professor Whatley. Fess's model served him well and Fundy advocated and maintained a similar discipline while active in Seattle's segregated musicians' union as its business agent.

William Funderberg became a union musician early while in high school, when he joined Birmingham's "Colored" Local 733, originally founded by Whatley and Ivory "Pops" Williams. This came about because the Birmingham Industrial School band played professional engagements. The band favored a "businessman's bounce" style which made them popular throughout the region. In so doing, William Funderberg joined a lengthy list of Birmingham Industrial School band members who became professional musicians. Fellow students went on to work in the orchestras of Duke Ellington, Count Basie, and that of fellow grad and Fess Whatley protégé Erskine Hawkins. As a young alto saxophonist, Fundy was known for having a "beautiful sound and for being a reader." Because of these talents and his strong business abilities, he was active with his and other bands in and around Birmingham until 1942. Fellow musician, Frank "Doc" Adams, recalled that Funderberg had the same reputation for high standards and "polish" in the way that he conducted himself and led his own big band. From its home base of Birmingham, Fundy's band played throughout Local 733's territory which extended all the way to Chattanooga. During World War II he was recruited for the segregated Navy big band based at Great Lakes Naval Facility, near Chicago. Following this he moved on to Seattle.

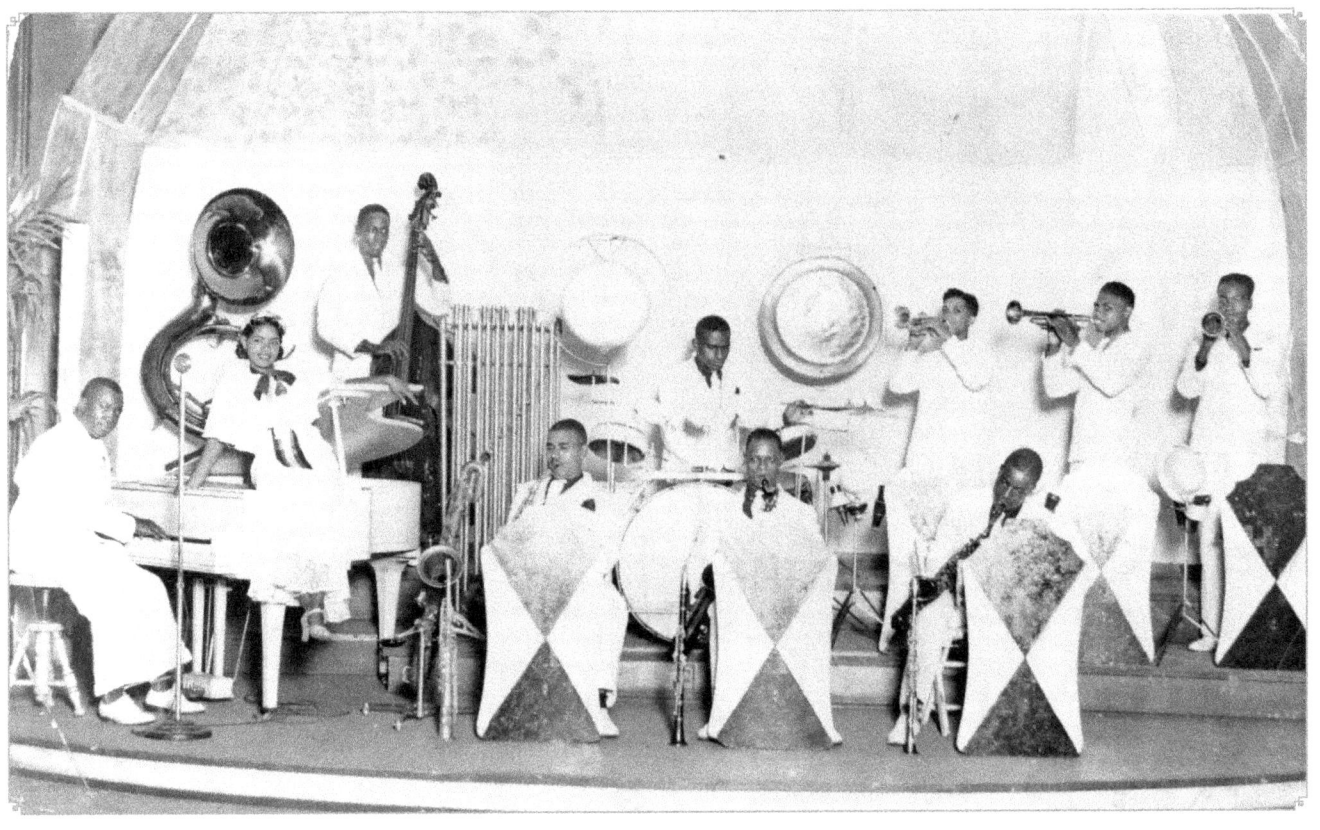

48.) William Funderberg Big Band, Birmingham, Alabama, 1941. L-R: Johnny L. Bell, piano; Bernice Bates, vocals; Nazareth J. Bogan Jr., bass and tuba; William Funderberg, baritone saxophone/leader; James "Cat Eye" Summerville, drums; unknown, bass clarinet; Johnny Grimes, trumpet; Luther Williams, alto saxophone; Johnny Grimes, Nelson Williams and unknown, trumpets.

Image provided by Birmingham, Alabama Public Library Archives.

Derniece Harris "Melody" Jones, pianist, organist, vocalist, band leader and 493 union woman, leads the band opposite. Born in Chicago in 1906, she moved first to Harrisburg, Pennsylvania, and after finishing high school on to Harlem in New York City. There she worked at one of Harlem's two black theaters, the Alhambra, where she played pipe organ for silent films. Shortly thereafter, she met stride piano legend and *raconteur par excellance* Thomas "Fats" Waller at New York's other black theater, the Lafayette, and later at rent parties. He offered her tips on her piano and organ playing, saying, "Whatever you do with your left hand, the right hand must make the melody stand out!" The young pianist took Waller's words to heart, crediting Waller for her name as well. Jones was a seasoned pro by the time this photograph was taken in 1945, shortly after moving to Seattle. In addition to her theater and cabaret work in New York, she was also a veteran of U.S.O. tours beginning in 1941, touring throughout the U.S., and then on to the Far East. As an early female instrumentalist, Jones also worked with another dynamic union woman. This was the drummer, vocalist, and club-owner Myrtle "Myrt" Francoise. Francoise and Jones fronted a popular local band called "Melody and Mirth." These two became role models for up-and-coming Seattle women who aspired to be professional musicians. (Patti Bown, pianist, composer and 493 member, described drummer Francoise as an early inspiration.) Melody Jones time as a leader was not without incident however, and she recalled losing jobs because she was not a light-skinned or "high yellow" female entertainer.

Her band was snapped performing at an undisclosed Jackson Street nightclub by veteran "On the Scene" photographer Al Smith. Indicative of the relaxed attitude towards union regulations, the institution of "The Kitty" was widespread as a "tip jar," and was often prominently displayed. Since it was against union regulations to accept tips, this practice was disparaged, and could result in fines if observed by 493's aforementioned business agent, baritone saxophonist and band leader William Funderberg.

49.) **Melody Jones, vocals and piano; Al Mitchell, guitar; Bob Marshall, bass; and The Kitty, 1945.** Al Smith photo.

The proprietor of the Washington Social Club, Sirless, "Sy" Groves is all smiles in the accompanying shot with famed dance troupe leader Katherine Dunham in this mid-1940s photograph. Earlier in 1937 Groves was a member of Seattle's Negro Repertory Company, a Federal Theater Project of the Works Progress Administration during the New Deal. Due to progressive themes, the WPA's Federal Theater Project had a short run, and by 1939 it was shut down for its allegedly Communist sympathies. In addition to an artistic streak, Groves was a tough businessman who usually landed on his feet. At the onset of World War II Groves, like many other Seattle blacks, worked in Bremerton in the shipyards. Following a failed attempt at a youth club on Union Street, he hit upon the successful formula for the Washington Social and Educational Club and located it at 23rd Avenue and East Madison. His niece Francis Demisse explained,

> *They had membership clubs. To get in you had to make a donation. Patti Bown said she used to go up the stairs and the stairs were creaky. They used to come up the back stairs, and they paid the policeman to get in. Everybody made money but the family..."*

A man of some contradictions, Groves was known to be tough with the dollar, particularly when it was time to pay his hired musicians. Ms. Demisse recalled a down-on-his-luck Lester, the "President of the Tenor Saxophone" Young, "beggin' Uncle Sy" for his money. In a vicious circle, Groves refused to pay Young until the end of a six-week stint at his club in 1948. Groves feared that Young once paid would promptly depart, and that his venue would lose money. Trumpeter and 493 man, Floyd Standifer also recalled threatening to take his pay in glassware if Groves did not pay up. Others such as Melody Jones, and a female drummer named Ruth Reimer worked at the venerable club. In the words of Demisse, "Sy used to keep everybody workin'."

> *One of those so employed was family member Viola Howell, who'd done shows as a teenaged dancer all around Seattle at the Palomar, the Colonial, and the Ford theaters. Howell recalled how a typical evening shift at the Washington Social Club went,*

"We'd open at 9:00 pm. Nine until 3:00 am, because I used to dance there too – entertain and wait tables... We had costumes, because I danced with a trio, my sister was the leader. Then there was Verna Mae and Eileen."

50.) Sy Groves and Katherine Dunham at the Washington Social Club, c. mid-1940s.
Photo courtesy of Francis Demisse.

Bebop pianist, composer, and accompanist, Gerald Wiggins came to Seattle unwillingly at 22, courtesy of the U.S. Army during World War II. In 1944 the draft caught up with the New York native and veteran of the 52nd Street scene, while he was on the bandstand with Benny Carter. Stationed at Fort Lewis, Wiggins' next gig was with the Twenty Ninth Special Services band, whose commanding officer and bandleader was Ernie Harper. Other band members included fellow 493 members Junior Raglin on bass, Wyatt Ruther on trombone, and Louis Jones on trumpet. Ever charming, "Wig" was given light duties in this Army band, only having to play at the USO Club on Saturday night. After that he was free to play in Seattle where he was a much in-demand bebop piano player. He remained in the Emerald City until the end of the war and stuck around until 1948 with only a brief trip back to New York. Wig played at various clubs and had fond memories of working alongside other Emerald City stalwarts and 493 union members like Gerald Wells, Milton Green, Al Larkins, Vernon Brown, Emmet Lewis, John Marshall, and Al Pierre among others. He was also a favorite of local impresario Norm Bobrow, who featured him in various shows. At one point the fleet-fingered pianist lived just around the corner from the Washington Social Club. Possessed of immense talent and self-confidence, Wig wowed the locals nightly from 1:30-3:30 a.m. with an ability to perform while simultaneously reading. Questioned about this, he demurred, "Oh, those were just comic books." Additionally, Wig remembered that the Washington Social Club was a place where, "You bought a set up and then brought your own bottle... However, there was a lot of bootlegging going on, believe me. They had one guy called him, 'The Nerve Lifter.' (Smiling.) Yeah, The Nerve Lifter. Call him and he'd bring a pint of whatever you wanted."

The pianist didn't think much about the fact then that New York City's Musicians' Union Local 802 was integrated at this time, while Seattle had dual unions. "Hey, it was a sign of the times. That's the way it was. Nobody really complained about it, 'cause, like I say, that's the way it was. Didn't do you any good to argue. In fact, a lot of guys said with the amalgamation here (in Los Angeles, his home) they didn't want it. They thought it was going to keep 'em from getting jobs. But as it was, it opened up more jobs for them."

51.) Gerald Wiggins at the Teatro Romano, Verona, Italy in 1986.
Photo courtesy of Gerald Wiggins.

Clarence Williams, shown opposite at the microphone singing with the Leon Vaughn band, was a popular attraction at the Washington Social Club. The blues vocalist and guitarist was influenced by Aaron Thibeaux "T-Bone" Walker and gained a respectable Seattle following performing "Kansas City riffs and Texas Longhorn blues," as well as his version of the great Charles Brown hit, "Drifting Blues." Prior to this, Williams had made a name for himself in rooms like the Gaiety and the Club Alabam on Central Avenue in Los Angeles, alongside jazz musicians like saxophonists Jay McNeely, Tom Archia, and Maxwell Davis. Shown here at Seattle's Basin Street club, Williams was also a frequent performer at other Seattle rooms until 1949 when the Washington State legislature passed Bill 171 making alcohol legal in clubs. At that point "the Prince of the Blues" departed for Portland, Oregon where he became a popular jazz and blues fixture, remaining there for decades. Seattle locals like the young Quincy Jones along with Floyd Standifer, both of whom were in the big band of Bumps Blackwell, all got a chance to work at the Washington Social Club as well. National bands such as those of Lionel Hampton, Count Basie, Jimmie Lunceford, and the Will Mastin trio featuring a then unknown vocalist and dancer named Sammy Davis, Jr. dropped by too.

As far as membership in Local 493 went, later records indicate that only Vaughn and Aaron Davis from this particular quintet remained in the union through 1958 when the amalgamation with Local 76 took place. Both men joined the black musicians' union in 1943.

52.) **Blowing the Blues Away. L-R Ralph Stephens, Leon Vaughn, Aaron Davis, Clarence Williams, and Milton Walton, 1948 at Basin Street.** Al Smith photo.

Dance acts were also popular at the Washington Social Club. Shown here is an Emerald City favorite, "Princess Zenobia" Jefferson at another venerable institution, the Black and Tan nightclub, circa the 1940s. Zenobia danced at various Seattle venues including the Washington Social Club, along with the black Elks Club and Session's Playhouse, where she performed with Billy Tolles band. Arriving in town with her saxophonist husband Noble Perkins, who'd played with Fats Waller and Jimmie Lunceford, Zenobia went through some tough early times and helped her husband get his horn out of hock. Additionally, she washed and ironed stage uniforms for Perkins and "that blind boy," Ray Charles, who arrived in Seattle in 1948. Zenobia was not smitten with Charles, a 493 union man, asserting that he left town owing her money and never made any efforts to pay her back. Zenobia was resourceful though, and her charm considerable. She seemed to have worked her share and got by as a dancer during the era. Francis Demisse remembered a memorable evening involving some questionable billing as well as an animal act with Zenobia:

> "Uncle Sy wanted to have a 'New York Revue.' And here everybody came, everybody came to see the 'New York Revue.' And [all the dancers were] from Seattle. That's the truth, but he called it a 'New York Revue.' [Some of the audience said] 'That's Hattie Bee and Viola. That ain't no New York Revue.'

> "...I know more about the club because I helped my mother a lot with the food. My aunt was in the checkroom, my sister was waitin' tables. And Uncle Sy would be up there... One time he was even in one of the floor shows. Beauty and the Beast *with Zenobia, I think. I tell you he put on an ape costume (laughs) and I was laughin' so hard, it's a miracle you know.*"

53.) Princess Zenobia Jefferson dances at the Black & Tan, circa 1940.
Al Smith photo.

This playbill provides a look at the variety of acts which performed at the Washington Social & Educational Club. For this booking the room featured the jungle exotica of "Princess De Paur & Toulae" ("from Tahiti") and their "Tahitian Voo Doo Dancers." Jazz and blues came courtesy of Seattle bandleaders and presumed Local 493 members Al Hickey and Clarence Williams.

54.) Washington Social & Educational Club Playbill, circa 1946.
Club flyer courtesy of Jacqueline E. A. Lawson.

Al Hickey's Jive Bombers make up the final, Washington Social Club photo in this series. The Bombers, here in civilian guise, were regulars at the venue and are depicted with Duke Ellington's ace trumpeter Rex Stewart, who was in town with the Ellington band for a 1946 Seattle performance. John Willis, shown here on alto sax and a 493 officer for many years, recalled,

"We were up at the Washington Social club with Hickey's band. We didn't need to rehearse too much since we'd all been in the Navy together and had played in the after hours joints too. At the Washington Social Club, we were workin' 12 midnight to 5:00 AM, horrible hours. When I first started, I thought I was gonna die. Almost fell asleep at 2:00 AM... That lasted real well for a year, 1946."

Pianist Kenny Boas, who was Caucasian and a Local 493 man, amplified on this theme,

"I played there in '46 and '47 with the Jive Bombers. Funny things you remember. It was the morning and the sun would come up and they'd close the shades...

"Clarence Williams would be walkin' out singin' the blues. He was great. A lot of musicians came through and sat in... We'd be playing there and people'd be drinking. They're not necessarily drunk, but once they drank a certain amount of alcohol you could feel an electric atmosphere... And the longer we played, like their minds were together. Seems to create a feeling over the whole group. It's like a Third Mind, that feeling. And it would feel so good that we would play longer than we were supposed to. That's where they'd do that deal where they'd pull the shades down to keep the sun out."

55.) Al Hickey's Jive Bombers at the Washington Social & Educational Club, c. 1946. L-R: Harry "Doc" Wheeler, trumpet; Rex Stewart, trumpet; Ralph Davis, drums; Al Hickey, tenor saxophone; and John Willis, alto sax. Photo courtesy of Ralph Davis. Note the ubiquitous Kitty on the bandstand.

The smiling countenance in this photo belongs to Seattle booking agent, bandleader, and nominal vibraphonist Robert "Bumps" Blackwell, posing here with an unknown, but equally happy vocalist. Bumps was born in Seattle in 1918 into a musical family which also included brother Charles, who became a renowned drummer. Bumps soon established himself as an agent for various Seattle bands, running the business out of a swinging butcher shop at 23rd and Madison. Both he and his brother were members of Local 493. Bumps probably observed 493 contract minimums since his name only appeared once in union minutes for a dispute with white bandleader and Local 76 member, Bob Harvey. Blackwell's part in Seattle's jazz history is enshrined thanks to his work with the Charlie Taylor band. Renamed as the Bumps Blackwell Junior Band, it featured a young Quincy Jones, Buddy Catlett, and Floyd Standifer among others. At one point in the late 1940s Blackwell had a virtual lock on many of Seattle's jazz gigs and most of Seattle's jazz players, including a 17-year-old Ray Charles, all worked for him. For example, on July 28, 1945, Bumps and orchestra were featured at Civic Auditorium in a "Swingsational" Battle of the Bands, playing favorites like "In the Groove" and "Red Hot Jive." Vern Mallory and his orchestra rounded out the bill, advertised as one of "Ellis Coder's Civic Dances." Although Blackwell never achieved household name recognition, no less an authority than Quincy Jones credits him as having a "great ear for talent." Leaving Seattle in the mid-1950s for Los Angeles, Blackwell soon produced successful recordings for Lou Rawls, the gospel group the Soul Stirrers, and Sam Cooke. During this time, at a garage studio on 28th Street in L.A. with jazz drummer Roy Porter, Blackwell recorded a then-unknown, singing piano player named Richard Penniman from Macon, Georgia. Based on this demo, Blackwell took Penniman, a.k.a. "Little Richard," to New Orleans. There he produced records of Little Richard for Art Rupe's Specialty Records using some of the Crescent City's finest R&B players. Little Richard's trademark, "Tutti Frutti" came out of these sessions, and rock and roll was never the same.

56.) Robert "Bumps" Blackwell and vocalist, c. 1949.
Photo courtesy of Ernie Hatfield.

Besides the bustling club scene during this era, radio helped popularize jazz for Seattle residents. As mentioned earlier, by 1925 white Local 76 functionaries had locked up most playing rights at stations like KFOA and excluded Local 493 members, except for Gerald Wells' live KOL broadcasts. Other mentions of Emerald City broadcasts during this time for black members of the musicians' union appear to be non-existent. The matter is complicated however, since the non-union Filipino musician, Frank Molina, played KJR live broadcasts during the 1930s. Additionally, saxophonist and bandleader Joe Darensbourg had his own program at KXA broadcasting "twice a week" during this era.

A decade later jazz was arguably the popular music of the day and there was plenty of black content on radio – both nationally and locally. Greats like Ella Fitzgerald, shown opposite circa 1942 with The Four Keys, sang hits then on radio such as "All I Need Is You," "Mama Come Home," and "Fuji Boo." Fitzgerald turned professional in 1934, winning first place at the Apollo Theater's "Amateur Night in Harlem" competition. From there the young orphan became famous with the great drummer and bandleader Chick Webb. She hit big in 1938 with the million seller, "A-Tisket, A-Tasket," and went on to lead Webb's big band for two years from 1939-1941 after the drummer's death of tuberculosis. In this publicity still, soon to be local pianist and 493 union stalwart, Ernie Hatfield is shown second from left, with Ella and the Four Keys.

57.) Ella Fitzgerald and the Four Keys, c. 1942. L-R: Bill Furness, piano; Ernie Hatfield, vocals and drums; Slim Furness, guitar; Ella, vocals; Peck Furness, bass. Photo courtesy Ernie Hatfield collection.

A list of players in Seattle during this period reflects a thriving music scene and reads like a Who's Who of international and local jazz greats. Consider this sampling from 1942-1946: Lucky Millinder and Noble Sissle; Cab Calloway; Palmer Johnson and Russell Jones; Al Pierre; Jimmie Lunceford; Fletcher Henderson; Louis "Satchel Mouth" Armstrong; Saunders King; Ernie Fields; Earl "Fatha" Hines; Coleman Hawkins, Sister Rosetta Tharpe, Eddie Durham and his All Girl Orchestra, along with another all-female band for which Durham wrote arrangements, the International Sweethearts of Rhythm; and a certain Thomas Wright "Fats" Waller. The latter is shown opposite in two views with trademark grin: one from a 1936 Mills Music ad and another performing at the Moore Theater during a "coast-to-coast twelve weeker" national tour. The Seattle show was on a Sunday June 13th, 1941 for a jovial interracial crowd. Appearing two years before his untimely death at 39 in Kansas City, this show's producer was Norm Bobrow. By arrangement with Bobrow's friend, A.F.M. 493 President Gerald Wells, Waller played another Seattle date the next night at the "Senator's Ball Room" at Seventh Avenue and Union Street. The show was billed as a Local 493 event, utilizing mixed hyperbolic, wartime metaphors as "...one of the greatest musical and dance blitzkriegs ever waxed in the U. S. A."

Ernie Hatfield, touring with Ella Fitzgerald then, reminisced about an earlier triple bill he was on with Ella along with Fats, and Erskine Hawkins, the latter famous for such hits as "After Hours," "Tippin' In," and "Tuxedo Junction." Hatfield explained about the Springfield, Massachusetts show:

"We all got there kind of early, so to kill the time we said let's have a little penny ante crap game – ten cents, five cents. So, Fats had the dice. He rolled the dice, but before they stopped he says, 'Hedy Lamarr,' and then he rolled an eight. He picked 'em up again and he threw 'em out. And he says, 'Lena Horne.' He threw a five. Picked 'em up and rolled 'em. Before he had a chance to say any-thing, Erskine Hawkins says, 'Hattie McDaniel,' and he crapped out (laughs). Then [Fats] says 'Damn. Gone With the Wind!'"...

58.) Fats Waller Plays Seattle 1941, Moore Theater. Al Smith photograph.

Traveling, dues-paying bands were an important source of income for Local 493. When out-of-town black bands like these played Seattle, they usually fed 493's coffers by paying work dues, bringing in much-needed revenue. The International Sweethearts of Rhythm were members of the American Federation of Musicians' union and were a rare all-female interracial band which played the Negro touring circuit throughout the country during the 1940s. During World War II the military draft decimated the ranks of the country's traditionally all-male big bands. This situation provided work for various "all girl" groups. Some of these included the International Sweethearts, as well as the black All-Star Girl Orchestra of Texas-born Eddie Durham. Both bands played concerts in Seattle in 1944. With parallels to "Rosie the Riveter" in Seattle's bustling World War II economy, the International Sweethearts toured frequently and were surely a source of race and gender pride to Seattle women in Local 493, the African American community, and others.

The International Sweethearts originated from the Piney Woods School in Mississippi, traveling internationally as a swing big band from 1940-1949. The term "International" in the band's name served as a protective cover for band members who were black, white, Chinese, and Mexican. According to leader Anna Mae Winburn, "We had so many mixed girls, mulattas..." as well as white alto player Roz Cron, who was coached to describe herself as "mixed." Such a covert line up resulted in frequent run-ins with the police, though not in Seattle. "So, we had quite a time," Winburn noted, "we did a lot to break down prejudice in the South." The band also helped shatter the myth, commonly repeated in the literature, that female musicians couldn't play. Defying this stereotype, the Sweethearts swung hard. For example, this "all girl group" were popular favorites of the discerning audiences at the Apollo Theater in Harlem, and from 1941 to 1945, they performed at the venue as much as, or more than, their male counterparts.

59.) International Sweethearts of Rhythm in Seattle, c. 1944. L-R: Leader Anna Mae Winburn conducting; Willie Mae Wong, baritone saxophone; Roz Cron, alto saxophone; Helen Saine, alto sax; Grace Bayron, tenor sax; and Pauline Brady, drums. Al Smith photo.

Following are two views of vocalist and Local 493 man Russell Jones. On the next page in the photograph below, he is shown singing at the Union Club. Possessed of a strong baritone voice, Jones was a perennial Seattle favorite, usually in tandem with the "King of the Boogie Woogie piano," Palmer Johnson, who may be obscured behind him here. The act also did well at clubs in Portland and Vancouver, B.C. Jones, a "table singer," was originally from Los Angeles. He arrived in Seattle in the 1930s and stayed on as a popular mainstay during the 1940s, working extensively with local bandleader Al Pierre. Fellow 493 unionists Ralph Davis at the trap drums and Local President, Gerald Wells on tenor can also be identified in this band photograph.

A publicity photo of Jones with partner Palmer Johnson above offers another view of the singer. This shot appeared as part of a local performance promotion on October 14, 1942 in Seattle's black community newspaper, the *Northwest Enterprise.* In a special "Flash" to "all service men in and near Seattle," the paper publicized a stint at the Palomar Theater the following week by Johnson and Jones.

PALMER JOHNSON AND RUSSELL JONES

Here they are folks, Palmer Johnson, King of the Boogie Woogie Piano keyboard, and Russell Jones the bronze Lawrence Tibbitt of the Northwest. They are packing them in at the Palomar this week, so go down and give the home boys a hearty cheer. Palmer is featuring "Peer Gynt Suite" in swing, from Anitras Dance. You will have to hear it to really appreciate this new swing arrangement by Palmer himself. Russel Jones is freezing the audience in their seats at each performance, with "Martha," "Road to Mandalay," and "All the Things You Are." Russell was never better, and his interpretation of All the Things You Are really does something to you. These two boys are wonderful and must be classed as first rate entertainers in a class by themselves. Don't miss seeing the act. The Northwest Enterprise's stamp of approval is placed on the program the boys are presenting at the Palomar this week.

60.) Two views of Russell Jones: (above) Singing at the Union Club, c. 1944, with: Ralph Davis, drums; Gerald Wells, tenor saxophone; possibly Al Larkin, bass; unknown, alto sax; and possibly Palmer Johnson piano. Al Smith photo, and a *Northwest Enterprise* ad. **(top left) with Palmer Johnson,** courtesy of University of Washington Libraries.

115

The next three photographs and accompanying advertisements from the *Northwest Enterprise* provide a visual for some of the many national acts to perform in Seattle during the early World War II years. Top 1940s attractions like Louis Armstrong, Cab Calloway, Duke Ellington, Lucky Millinder, and Noble Sissle gave locals plenty of high quality music. And their bands generally pumped much-needed revenue into Local 493's coffers. In addition to paying work dues to the Local, traveling bands also paid through another time-honored, union mechanism known as "featherbedding." As mentioned earlier, this practice dictated that traveling bands had to add local musicians to play certain rooms. This was so even if they did not use any local players, paying the difference to the Local. All of this kept black 493's head above water. Additionally, the union saved rent money by locating its office at 401 – 409 19th Avenue East. This was the home of Gerald and Elizabeth Dean Wells for most of the 1940s. During this period Gerald Wells was 493's president, an in-demand saxophonist, and concert promoter.

61.) Louis Armstrong plays Seattle May 19, 1942. Photo courtesy of University of Washington Libraries, Special Collections.

62.) Cab Calloway in town October 23, 1943. Photo courtesy of University of Washington Libraries.

63.) Duke Ellington, circa 1943. Photo courtesy of University of Washington Libraries.

64.) Lucky Millinder "The Maestro" at Finnish Hall and the Noble "Sultan of Swing" Sissle Orchestra at the Palomar, September 1943.
Northwest Enterprise ads courtesy University of Washington Libraries.

Oakland blues and torch singer Dee Dee Hackett, shown opposite, moved to Seattle during the bustling good times of the 1940s. She fit right in at places like the Union Club, Two Pals, and Yukon Club, all part of the territory or turf controlled by Local 493. Hacket appeared regularly with pianist, 493 leader and venue owner Al Pierre, back to camera in this shot. Other definite members shown here include drummer Vernon Brown, and Al Marshall. The popular singer was at home in a variety of contexts and thrived on "singing up a storm... way up tempo and she was out there scatting" according to boogie woogie piano man, Palmer Johnson. Fellow musicians recalled her as an accomplished vocalist, who originally learned her trade in the church. Another singer and 493 member, Russell Jones mentioned that she "could sing all them nasty songs," an asset with the rougher club, armed forces, and working class crowds. Seattle fans loved the vocalist and no doubt danced to her "way up tempo" jazz and blues repertoire.

65.) Dee Dee Hackett's Naughty Blues. L-R: Al Hickey in Army uniform, tenor sax; Al Marshall in Navy uniform, bass; Vernon Brown, trap drums; and Al Pierre, piano; circa 1944 - 1945. Al Smith photo.

The jitterbug dance first hit in 1934. At that time, Cab Calloway had just recorded "The Jitterbug." The song was written by his trumpeter Edwin Swayzee, who'd heard trombonist, drummer and arranger, Harry Alexander White, a.k.a. Father White, use the term. At Benny Goodman's career-enhancing 1934 Palomar performance in Hollywood, newspapers reported on the "jitterbugging" done there and a 20-year dance craze ensued. The dance was particularly popular on the integrated dance floor of the Savoy Ballroom in Harlem. As depicted in the next two photographs, the action in Seattle appears to be at a World War II era jitterbug contest, then in vogue. This was not always the case and in the earlier days of the Swing Era, "most dance floors did not permit jitterbugging." Only a few years after these shots in the 1950s, Dick Clark would not allow the dancers on his American Bandstand show to perform jitterbugging with "aerials, lifts, dips, partnered Charlestons, or jazz moves." In the second illustration, note the rather diverse make up of the audience, some of whom seem a bit perplexed at the dancers' moves. Live bands played for "jitterbuggers," and by extension, 493 members may have provided the inspiration for these dancers.

Band leader, tenor sax ace, and Local 493 stalwart Billy Tolles fondly recalled the importance and commercial potential of dance in an era prior to when jazz became a sedentary, concert activity.

> *"Before I even started playing music, we had a jitterbug team that was one of the best on the West Coast. While we were dancing, people would be throwing money on the floor."*

66.) Jitterbugging Seattle, circa 1944.
Al Smith photographs.

Amid plentiful work and attendant good times for black unionists, white Local 76 administrators got tough about union regulations. Over the course of several months in 1945 many disciplinary actions took place. One instance involved 19-year old piano man Kenny Boas. Fed up with 76, the white bopper had already joined Local 493. Shortly thereafter Boas was brought up on multiple charges by his former union and eventually fined $100 for working without a contract. Another 76 action involved Charlie Blackwell, a top-drawer drummer who went on to work with jazz heavies such as Art Tatum, Count Basie, and Dave Brubeck among others. Blackwell, who was also a bandleader and brother of producer Bumps Blackwell, received a 76 fine for reporting late to work at the Aragon ballroom. Charges were brought by Local 76 man, Arthur Benson, who was described as "part owner of the Aragon." This turf wars action got Blackwell fined and deprived him of his contracting privileges at the Aragon.

In another recorded action, Local 76 placed the Black and Tan night spot on its "forbidden territory" list in June 1945, as part of a larger battle about off limits clubs. The listing was for repeated union room work rule violations, forbidding African American *and* white union members from performing at or patronizing the club. 493 President Gerald Wells appeared before the Local 76 Board, which decided to write to A. F. of M. International President James Caesar Petrillo for clarification on the issue. Petrillo may have offered a suitable compromise to the two musicians' unions, since at the time of this 1946 photograph the venue, billing itself as "Colored Waiters, Porters and Cooks Club, Inc.," appears to be thriving. Former black Elks Club waitress Dorothy Lomax is visible standing clad in black, with beaming smile and wearing a black hat, fifth from left in back row.

67.) One Night at the Black & Tan, circa 1946.
Photo courtesy of Dorothy Lomax.

Drummer Merle Fuller is shown in this 1944 photograph with a quartet at the venerable Club Rizal. Located in the heart of the International District, the club named for the Philippine revolutionary martyr, poet and physician Jose Rizal, who lived from 1861-1896, was a popular music and multi-purpose venue, and was a hub for local Filipinos. One time Seattle resident and author Carlos Bulosan wrote a cataclysmic scene set there, thinly disguising it as the "Manila Dance Hall" in his heartbreakingly honest 1943 novel, *America Is In The Heart*. Also note on the wall behind the musicians, the crossed flags of the Philippines and the United States.

Fuller was advertised as an "Ace Drummer" and was the leader of the band. Guitarist Milt Green was also popular during the era and went on to steady work as a leader of his own groups, playing in a style influenced by guitar legend Charlie Christian and the piano playing of Nat "King" Cole. Vocalist and tenor saxophonist Tootie Boyd (famous for high-speed, high jinks on the drive to Portland according to Gerald Wiggins,) along with pianist Ralph Stephens round out the band. Although Local 493 union membership records are spotty during this period, when a final list was published in 1958 only Green remained in the union.

68.) **Merle Fuller Quartet at the Club Rizal, 1944. L-R Fuller, Milt Green, Tootie Boyd, and Ralph Stephens.** Al Smith photo.

Mid-year 1946 found Seattle impresario, KXA radio personality, jazz crusader, and fervent integrationist Norm Bobrow producing a "Northwest All-Star Swing Concert." The former New Yorker was a charismatic champion of the music, who'd earlier been at the University of Washington with pianist Jimmy Rowles. He is also well regarded for producing Seattle's first swing concert in 1940. Bobrow was a friend to many Local 493 members and its President Gerald Wells. He is also credited with bringing jazz to the attention of mainstream white Seattle audiences. Despite his good intentions, or perhaps because of them, during the time when he ran his own Continental and Players clubs, Bobrow also drew Local 76 official's ire. At the Players in 1946 he was fined by white Local 76's business agent for allowing Local 493 musicians to jam without paying them. In Bobrow's defense, this was a common infraction, which was mostly enforced by Local 76 against black 493 union members.

The following two photographs highlight Bobrow's concert at the Metropolitan Theatre. Band personnel illustrate the complexities of dual unionism in Seattle. In the photograph, there is an up-and-coming 17-year-old vocalist by the name of Ernestine Anderson. An internationally acclaimed singing sensation, Anderson never joined Seattle's Black Musicians' Union, preferring membership in Actors Equity Association. Guitarist Al Turay, a self-described "Big Swede" and lifetime member of Local 76, was a fellow traveler with 493 musicians, who loved to sit in at black after-hours sessions in Jackson Street clubs. Also noteworthy is the guitarist and bassist Bill Rinaldi, who'd switched allegiances in the 1930s, becoming the first Caucasian to join Local 493. Other 493 regulars in this interracial band include trumpeter Bob Russell, and tenor sax stalwart Jabo Ward.

69.) Norm Bobrow's Northwest All-Star Concert, 1946. L-R: Al Turay, guitar; Ira "Skeets" Savill, drums; Bill Rinaldi, bass; Ernestine Anderson, vocals; Jabo Ward, tenor saxophone; and Bob Russell, trumpet. Photo courtesy Al Turay.

70.) Program for Norm Bobrow's "Northwest All-Star Swing Concert," 1946. Courtesy Al Turay.

The following photographs provide a window into more of the clubs which Seattle's segregated Musicians' Local 493 controlled as part of its territory. Additionally, these shots spotlight the local musicians, all trade unionists, who played there and the club denizens who made the scene possible. Fleet-fingered pianist, vibraphonist, and 493 man, Elmer Gill, shown here at the Union Club, fondly recalled an era of full employment for black professional musicians. He remembered when he and other young musicians could improve their skills by illegally jamming with the likes of the Count Basie or Ellington big bands at the Rocking Chair club or with Satchmo at Todd's. After a stint in the Army band at Fort Lewis, Gill broke into the Seattle music scene and got his first professional gig at the Rocking Chair, located on 14th just off Yesler. He explained about his time there,

> *"Man, sometimes we'd be playing the blues. We'd start in playing at 12 o'clock and at 4:00 in the morning we'd still be playing the same blues... The thing would be moving like everything. Everybody would come up and take their turn singing or playing... I learned a lot of tunes in there, you know I had never heard, 'cause I didn't know nothing about jazz really. I hadn't thought much about it."*

71.) At the Union Club, circa 1947. L-R: Bob Russell, trumpet; Al Hickey, tenor saxophone; Bob Braxton, alto sax; Ralph Davis, drums; and Elmer Gill, piano; unknown fans standing. Photo courtesy Ralph Davis.

72.) Good Times at the Rocking Chair, circa mid-1940s.
Al Smith photo.

73.) **Pops at Todd's on Jackson Street, circa 1945-46. L-R: Vernon Brown, Louis Armstrong, Terry Cruise, Bob Russell, Ralph Davis, and Mary Brooks, wife of pianist Len Brooks.** Photo courtesy Ralph Davis.

74.) Al Hickey band at the Spinning Wheel, circa 1946. L-R: Al Larkin, bass; Dave Bradford, trumpet; Ralph Davis, drums; John Moton, piano; Al Hickey, tenor sax; and Bob Braxton, alto. Photo courtesy Ralph Davis.

75.) Playing the Club Lido, circa mid-1940s. L-R: unknown, drums; Bill Rinaldi, bass; Al Turay, guitar; unknown, bass; Bob Braxton, alto saxophone; and Eddie Diamond, piano. Photo courtesy Al Turay.

By today's standards this wide-open club world, which Seattle's famed "tolerance" policy and a strong economy fostered, is hard to fathom. Guitarist and Local 493 fellow traveler, Al Turay summed it up well,

> *"During this time, you worked a lot of places five or six nights a week. Different scene than it is now. Go into a club and stay there as a rule for six months. You could play every night. Now a steady gig is working two weeks, just Saturday nights."*

Though Turay may be exaggerating about working every night, which is technically in violation of union work rules, these must have been heady days. Al Hilbert grew up in this world, singing for spare change during the 1920s with Al Pierre in downtown Seattle. Hilbert on other occasions in 1929 drove his grandmother Edythe Turnham and her Black Hawks band in a flat bed truck with the band playing, a la New Orleans "tail gating," promoting their next gig. Dorothy Hilbert recalled her husband Al's extracurricular activities at various rooms during the 1940s.

> *"He managed the Main Event and also worked for Dave Lee at the Basin Street – ran the card games there. He also ran the crap table at The 908, and Wanda Brown was a shill for him. Yeah, Dave Beck and all those [Teamster] guys used to come in there. Dave Beck lost a boat load there one time..."*

Ms. Hilbert was just as outspoken about the tolerance policy which allowed for the wide-open atmosphere of Seattle's jazz club demi-monde. Recalling her employment at the Yukon Club on Jackson Street she said,

> *"That was a really neat place to work. They would call us up and let us know when they were going to raid. Then everybody would be very careful and if the night bartender had taken the raid the night before, he'd call the day bartender and tell him to come down and take this one. The customers didn't even know that they were there, y'know. They just kept on drinkin'. Well, it was a tolerance policy. Payoffs and all."*

76.) Tolerance & The Beat – mid-1940s. Ogawa photo courtesy of University of Washington Libraries.

Lionel Hampton gets plenty of air, opposite, at an interracial 1946 Seattle concert, where fans appear to be having almost as good a time as the maestro. Two years later Hampton hired a 15-year old Garfield high school student named Quincy Jones to go out on the road with him. However, Hamp's no-nonsense wife and manager, Gladys, nixed the deal telling Quincy to come back after he graduated from high school. In 1950 Hampton's white vocalist, and another Seattle resident, Janet Thurlow, reminded him of his promise and Quincy joined the integrated band after graduating. (Fellow segregated musicians' union member Elmer Gill was also in this fabled ensemble.) Hamp is often written off as an Uncle Tom for continuously touring the Jim Crow South during this period. However, in his defense, the vibes man recalled that he "cut the ropes down on the dance floor more than once, ..." a device which separated black and white dancers in the South. These actions, he believed, helped "soften them up through the years" until concerts and dances were eventually integrated.

The band's late, great saxophonist and flutist Jerome Richardson summed up Hamp's consumate skills with an audience:

> *"What Hampton did then, they call it rock and roll now. He'd crisscross America playing barns with sawdust on the floor, concert halls, clubs, jook joints – whatever it was – and he'd kill 'em. He'd pound that backbeat on two and four and I don't give a shit who you were, he rocked your ass until you got up on that floor and did the jigaboo. It was almost like jungle music. Pound that beat on two and four, just pound the natives into submission, till every single one of them hollered. He'd hit it till he saw pimps standing on oil drums dancing, people flipping each other doing the jitterbug, and every single person hollering, all that kind of stuff. Hamp was wild. He wanted that every night. He lived for that."*

77.) Flying Home With The Lionel Hampton Orchestra, Seattle Civic Auditorium, 1946. Al Smith photo, autographed by Hampton. Illinois Jacquet on tenor saxophone.

During the post war period, Local 493 enjoyed relative economic security. Fed by both resident musicians paying work dues on club jobs, and a host of traveling black bands, like Lionel Hampton's, the union enjoyed what was arguably its strongest period. Records indicate that a sort of rainbow coalition all called this union theirs. The predominantly black membership was joined by a small number of white boppers, and even Hawaiians beginning in the 1930s through the 1940s, as dues paying members of AFM Local 493. One of the many bands coming through then was the Jimmy White Trio, with whom eventual Seattle resident and 493 union musician Ernest Hatfield worked. Hatfield joined Seattle's segregated musicians' union in 1950, some time after leaving Ella Fitzgerald and Philadelphia where he'd been a member of that city's segregated musicians' union, Local 274. Hatfield came west with guitarist and vocalist White and bassist Duke Johnson. The accompanying publicity still, ad, and clipping from a Eureka, California show provide visuals of the band. The easy-going piano man was matter of fact about paying work dues to the various unions in each city he toured, including New York's non-segregated Local 802. Examples from Hatfield's traveling book and work dues receipts follow, including a 493 entry signed by its secretary and alto sax man Bob Braxton. Of this West Coast tour Hatfield recalled a particular Walla Walla club incident where Jim Crow met the almighty dollar.

"... Jimmy White had a new Buick and we took turns driving... We drove to Omaha, Nebraska. Had breakfast there and then started out and landed in Utah. Ogden, Utah and then opened up in Walla Walla. This was at a club. They sold whiskey, beer, and everything. People were listening, the tables were pretty close together, there wasn't any dancing space in there. Then [the manager] told us he didn't want us to associate with any of the customers. But we had a man who lived next door to us in the motel we had. We didn't know him, but one day we were cooking. And the aroma was going all over the motel and this guy stuck his head out the door and said,... 'That smells good.' We said, 'Would you like to join us for dinner?' So, he brought his wife over, had dinner with us. Wanted to know where we were working and we told him.

"He came down there that night, and he was ordering drinks so fast for himself. Finally, he asked us to come down and sit with him at the table. So, Jimmy says, 'What the hell.' (Laughs.) We went and sat with him. Y'know what the manager said to us? 'I think it's alright that you fellas sit with him. You seem like nice fellas.' That wasn't it. Y'see this guy before he got ready to leave, he ordered a case of beer to take home. He spent money. [The manager] wasn't looking at color or anything. He was looking at green. (Laughs.) Yeah, he was looking at green. And from then on if anybody asked us to sit with them then everything was fine..."

78.) The Jimmy White Trio, circa 1949-1950. L-R: Duke Johnson, bass; White, guitar and vocals; and Ernie Hatfield at the piano. Photograph courtesy of Ernie Hatfield.

79.) Period ad and clipping for the Jimmy White Trio, circa 1950.
Courtesy of Ernie Hatfield.

80.) **Ernie Hatfield's Travelling Book from Philadelphia's segregated AFM Local 274, along with various work dues receipts including those from Walla Walla's Local 501, Pasco's 524, and Seattle's 493.** Courtesy of Ernie Hatfield.

Solid economic conditions continued during the post-war boom and gave the 50-100 dues-paying members of the black musicians' union a chance to branch out into a space of their own. Beginning in 1948, the Musicians' Protective Union Local 493 AFM was first headquartered at 1037 Jackson Avenue. Next, in 1951 it moved to 418a Second Avenue. In 1952 or 1953 the union settled into its final location at 1319 E. Jefferson, as can be seen in the accompanying illustration. In a small "clubhouse" atmosphere, it took on the name of "The Blue Note." There it alternatively conducted union business and featured non-stop, all-hours, weekend music and jam sessions. This happy, albeit somewhat chaotic way of doing union business, continued until 1956, the year the black and white unions merged. What the Capitol Hill room lacked in outward appearances or the stolid institutionalism of its mother Local downtown at 2620 Third Avenue, it more than made up for in camaraderie. At The Blue Note the musicians were the union's officers. They ran their union and club as they wanted. Though not speakeasy, it had a number of things in common with such rooms. It was a modest structure on a relatively quiet side street. The unpretentious building featured a bar, piano, drum kit on a small stage, bathrooms and a business office in the back. The center of the room featured a large, tiled black and white treble clef. Drinks were subsidized at 25-35 cents each. A young Buddy Catlett recalled that "you had to watch it not to get sauced out of your mind" at the clubhouse. On the plus side, he recalled improving his playing skills by working in bands at the club alongside local tenor titans such as Billy Tolles and Jabo Ward.

A high point of the friendships and camaraderie engendered at The Blue Note were the traveling "ringers" who came to jam there. Trumpet great Rex Stewart along with saxophonists Johnny Hodges and Ben Webster, who knew 493 men Terry Cruise and Vernon Brown from their previous work in Detroit and Minneapolis, all swung by. So did trumpet ace Thad Jones. Fellow trumpeter Floyd Standifer fondly recalled,

> "I first ran into Thad Jones and got to playin' with him and made the mistake of playin' over my head a bit. And he was with Basie... Whoa! But he wasn't that far ahead of me and we got to be friends after that..."

81.) Musicians' Protective Union, Local 493, AFM aka "The Blue Note," c. 1953, 1319 East Jefferson Street. Peter Blecha Collection.

82.) American Federation of Musicians' Local 493 Officers and stalwarts, circa 1953.
Courtesy of Ernie Hatfield.

More examples of Local 493 ephemera from 1953 and 1956 are shown here, in the form of piano man Ernie Hatfield's union cards. Signed by saxophonist and union secretary John Willis, they appear alongside Hatfield's 1949 and 1950 cards from Philadelphia's segregated Local 274. A dyed-in-the-wool unionist, Hatfield remained a stalwart in both the black and white Seattle musicians' associations for decades, as his later Local 76 cards confirm.

83.) Musicians' Unions Cards 1949-1976 from the segregated unions of Philadelphia and Seattle, and from integrated Seattle Local 76.
Courtesy of Ernie Hatfield.

When 17-year-old blind piano player and singer Ray C. Robinson came to Seattle in 1948 he was unknown. Most definitely, he was not yet what he was to become – an international sensation and multi-genre hit maker, Ray Charles. He arrived courtesy of a referral gig at the Black & Tan from 493 pianist and bandleader Derniece "Melody" Jones, who also paid for Mr. Ray Charles Robinson's Trailways bus ticket to Seattle from Tampa, Florida. Guitarist Garcia McKee, who knew the ambitious Robinson, arranged the trip. In the Emerald City Charles, then heavily influenced by Nat "King" Cole, joined McKee and bassist Milt Garred working Local 493 turf clubs as the Maxin or McSon Trio. The pianist and singer soon became a 493 member, remaining in the union until he moved to Los Angeles in the middle of 1950. He also kept current on his dues until the merger of Seattle's black and white musicians' unions in 1958, as did "Gossie" McKee, Garred, and Jones. Reports of Charles' abilities then vary, and Dorothy Hilbert recalled humble beginnings,

> *"Many years ago, there was a man here known as R.C. Louis Todd at the Black & Tan didn't hire him. My husband (Al Hilbert, club and gambling manager,) who ran the Main Event didn't hire him. So finally Big Lewis at The Rocking Chair or The Rose then... well, he hired him."*

Seattle's black newspaper, *The Northwest Enterprise*, mentions another performance of the time by R.C. Robinson, singing "in his solid style reminiscent of King Cole," and playing with "French and Be-Bop All Stars" at the Trianon June 19, 1949. The band featured a mysterious (European?) Julius MacVootie (using then current jive) along with Gerald and Buddy Brashear, Floyd Standifer, and "probably Al Larkins on bass," all 493 men. Eight months later, as these previously unpublished photographs attest, Charles worked a Valentine's Day dance at Fort Lawton along with another new arrival, vocalist Ernestine Anderson, as well as an obscure drummer named Private Clifford Radney.

84.) **Ray Charles Robinson with Private Clifford Radney at Service Club No. 2, February 14, 1950, Fort Lawton.** Sotero Collection, courtesy of the Seattle Public Library.

85.) **Ernestine Anderson and Ray Charles Robinson on Valentine's Day 1950 at Fort Lawton.** Sotero Collection, courtesy Seattle Public Library.

Times were changing across the nation and in Seattle as the next photograph shows. An historical moment occurred during this 1950 era when blacks and white could dance together. A band performs on the stage, shown previously at the Service Club in Fort Lawton, in the upper left of the photo. The original photograph is captioned, "They said it couldn't be done." It was taken by an unidentified photographer, possibly Marjorie Polk Sotero, who also served as Director of the 6th Army Service Club at nearby Camp Jordan.

The struggle for equality at Fort Lawton had been a long one. In 1909 the fort became the base for the all-black 25th Infantry Regiment. This was one of only four all-African American U.S. regiments, whose troops came to be known as "Buffalo Soldiers," a name given them by Great Plains Indians. Around 1917 during World War I, black men and women first gained employment at Fort Lawton, a step up from the domestic roles they had been relegated to in Seattle. But during the Second World War, black soldiers rioted at Fort Lawton. African American service men violently reacted to second class treatment on August 14, 1944. This was due to "humiliating treatment by the military and civilians" such as the blacks only Army policy of shoveling snow, and not being allowed to go off base to area taverns, clubs, and stores. In addition, Italian prisoners of war kept at Fort Lawton were allowed "lenient, congenial treatment," including access to area taverns and service dances. At the dances local girls, according to a *Seattle Times* article, "make a big fuss over the Italians." Following a night of drinking by both Italians, and blacks, who'd just been informed that they were to be sent overseas the next day, a riot broke out which resulted in the death of Guglielmo Olivotto, one of the Italian prisoners. Complicating the matter, was the fact that the Italians were not Fascists, had been drafted, and wanted nothing to do with the war. The inquest, however, was marred by numerous irregularities including destroyed and suppressed evidence. This included the exclusion of the charge that white MPs had been harassing the Italians for some time and were probably the ones who killed the young Italian soldier. Nevertheless, when the results of the court martial were announced 28 black soldiers were given convictions for lynching and expelled from the Army with dishonorable discharges. Some 63 years later in October of 2007 an Army ruling by the Board of Corrections of Military Records ruled that black soldiers involved in the incident "were unfairly denied access to their attorneys and to investigative records and should have their convictions overturned." The following year in July of 2008 justice was finally served in a "low-key ceremony" at Fort Lawton when "a senior Army official handed out certificates setting aside the (lynching) convictions and converting the discharges to honorable status..." That fall, Ron James, assistant secretary of the Army for manpower and reserve affairs, journeyed to see Roy Laine Montgomery in Park Forest, Illinois. Montgomery had declined to participate in the earlier ceremonies, and so the Army came to him "to apologize in person... with a reparations check and an honorable discharge." Montgomery died December 6, 2012 and was the last known surviving soldier of this group.

86.) First integrated dance at Service Club, Fort Lawton, circa 1950.
Sotero collection, courtesy Seattle Public Library.

One of the Seattle musicians, who also played at Fort Lawton was the young Patti Bown, who in 1944 played the Officer's Club at thirteen with Pops Buford's band. Ms. Bown was born in Seattle July 26, 1931. She came from a musical family, and Patti and three of her four sisters had perfect pitch. Although her mother could play the blues, she did not want her daughter to become a jazz musician. Bown was a natural at the piano, however. She grew up during a musically rich period alongside Quincy Jones, Floyd Standifer, and Ray Charles, who taught her how to accompany singers. She remembered,

> *"When I walked home from school, I passed the pool parlor and the Mardi Gras and they always had jazz playing. My mother was saying 'No!' but the music was sensuous and it said, 'Yes!'"*

In 1949 Ms. Bown received a music scholarship to attend Seattle University. She also studied at Cornish College of the Arts and the University of Washington. In 1952 she performed with the Seattle Symphony and had dreams of working with her sister Edith (who went on to marry jazz arranger Jerry Valentine,) as a piano duo. At 22 she was a full-fledged member of Seattle's black musicians' union, joining officially on December 27, 1953. When Bown joined 493 it was headquartered at the Blue Note, at 1319 East Jefferson Street. As mentioned, the clubhouse-style local, complete with bar and dance floor, became the go-to, after hours spot for fabled jam sessions. Here locals like Bown could learn their craft. In a fascinating arrangement, The Blue Note was both an administrative union hall and a cultural center for bebop music.

Departing for New York in the mid-1950s, Bown remained a union musician, and in Gotham, became a member of that city's AFM Local 802, never segregated. After at first scuffling in the Big Apple, she eventually performed with Quincy Jones, Gene Ammons, and Dinah Washington among others. In 1959 Columbia Records released the first of two albums she recorded thanks to a good word from Jones. "Patti Bown Plays Big Piano," featured the hard-swinging pianist in a trio setting with drummer Ed Shaughnessy of *Tonight Show* fame, and bassist Joe Benjamin. Following a year in Europe with Quincy Jones big band (see page 170 below,) she returned to New York where she worked as music director for Sarah Vaughan and Dinah Washington. In later years she performed at the Newport Jazz festival at Carnegie Hall, and at the Kennedy Center. She received a lifetime achievement award at the Mary Lou Williams Women in Jazz Festival. Ms. Bown died in 2008.

87.) Patti Bown at the Piano, circa 1958.
Photo from author's collection.

For Local 493 the 1950s were good years in their on-again, off-again battles with mother Local 76 and the record reports few violations or infractions. President Gerald Wells and other 493 officers successfully navigated a clear path through these often treacherous waters. Four Nine Three's Secretary Treasurer, John Willis, had also learned the Jim Crow ropes well and during this time successfully petitioned for 76 support in a work dispute involving the Thunderbird Club.

During this same period from 1954-1956, 493 musicians led the push to integrate the unions. Reflecting a changing national attitude, the first successful amalgamation of segregated musicians' unions occurred in 1953, when Los Angeles's black Local 767 merged with white Local 47. The mood struck Seattle, and Local 493's segregated musicians' union set up its own negotiating committee. Its members consisted of Gerald Wells, Frank Walton and Ruth Sykes. On white 76's side President Harry Read chose team members: "George Bovingdon – attorney and musician, Percy Johnson – sign painter and (bass) musician, and Powell Barnett – King County employee and musician." In an indication that it was becoming much harder to work as a full time musician, Local 76 musicians also worked two jobs. Additionally in a fascinating race wrinkle, African American and dual musicians' unionist Powell Barnett is now representing "white" Local 76.

One of the bright spots in the shrinking scene was Elmer Gill's Ebony Café. The entrepreneurial Gill established the successful formula he called "Jam For Breakfast" from 6:00 a.m. until 9:00 a.m. for Saturday morning shows. The gamble paid off and Gill's early Saturday shows ran from 1953 through 1956, frequently with block-long, entrance lines. Shown opposite is an Ebony Cafe advertisement for Gill and Bob Braxton's mixed race bands. Another photograph depicts a memorable morning when two ringers joined the jam. Unlike Los Angeles where, according to up-and-coming producer Norman Granz, musicians feared jamming because of union sanctions, Seattle's Local 493 either did not care or discreetly kept the lid on the practice.

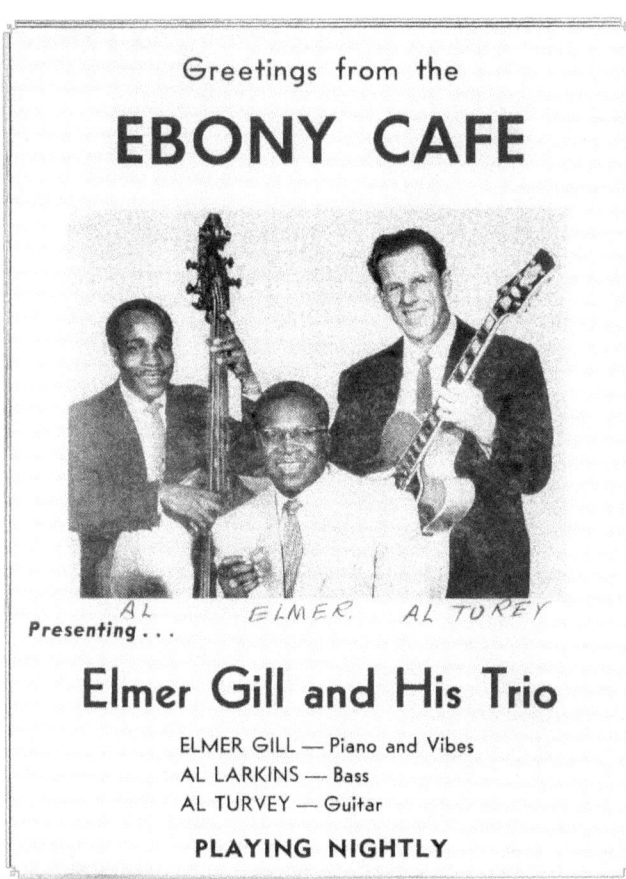

88.) Greetings from the Ebony Café, circa 1956. L-R Al Larkins, Elmer Gill, and Al Turay. Courtesy Ernie Hatfield.

89.) Breakfast Jam at the Ebony Café, circa 1956. L-R Percy Heath, Milt Jackson, Elmer Gill, and Al Turay. Courtesy Al Turay.

The stage was now set for the final push for the merger of Seattle's two musicians' unions, and by the end of 1954 they hammered out a proposal. This document detailed the formation of a holding committee for the disposition of Local 493 property. The matter remained at an impasse for two years however — whether due to economic or race reasons is unclear. Work fell off and musicians dropped out of the union as well. Even William Funderberg, Local 493's business agent, quit to make a better living on the docks. The baritone saxophonist and bandleader was against the merger with white 76, because he felt this would not benefit black musicians. Finally in 1956 a joint statement signed by Local 493 President Emmet Lewis and R. Dotson, Stan Payne, Frank Watson, and for 76 members Alvin Schardt, Ida B. Dillon, George Bovingdon, John Witwer, and Norman E. Houge notified the International of a "proposed amalgamation..." After receiving the green light from Local 76 at its General Meeting on November 13, 1956, the measure went before both unions for a vote on December 15, 1956. At the December meeting, Local 493 voted for amalgamation, but the vote was not unanimous. Elmer Gill voted against the merger, in earlier intra-union votes, as did William Funderberg. No black union records survive on the exact number of votes cast. However, Local 76 records show that 323 of their members voted in favor with 128 against. Two years later Local 493 disposed of its property and in early 1958 the two unions formally joined as one. Although the Local 76 publication, *Musicland* tried to allay fears, promising a better time for all with equal opportunities and an end to two-union price undercuts and favoritism, the reality was different. After amalgamation, the swift growth of rock and roll helped finish off jazz musicians' ability to earn a living. It was a case of too little too late. This merger also brought about the end of The Blue Note as a central meeting space for black pride, bebop jazz and a special union style. (See the mid-1990s photographs of the building which housed The Blue Note on the next page, followed by 1957 photos of 493's Ernie Hatfield and Stan Payne, along with Harold Redman.)

Whether The Blue Note collapsed simply due to attrition and changing times, or a combination of other factors is debatable. Ernie Hatfield remembered its downfall in detail, faulting 493 official John Freeman for letting the club's charter lapse. Hatfield's memory is corroborated by a January 19, 1959 story which details a police raid early at 2:00 AM Sunday on January 18, 1959 at "The Blue Note club at 1319 E. Jefferson" for "illegal liquor sales..." Hatfield believed The Blue Note never recovered from this raid explaining.

"I was at the Flame at that time [working with Floyd Standifer]... I wasn't goin' to go down [to The Blue Note] that night, my wife was with me. But the bartender had some friends from out of town – Oregon. They asked if I could get them in to The Blue Note. I wasn't interested, but o.k... We had just enough time to order one drink and the doors bust open and in came the cops. Raided the place... There were 56 of us, girls too, musicians and their wives. Took the girls in one paddy wagon, includin' my wife, and the fellas in another. Charged us each $10. I got out about three hours later. Some of 'em stayed in there till Sunday, that was Saturday night. So that was the end of The Blue Note."

90.) The Author at The Blue Note location, 1319 E. Jefferson, May 1996.
Photo courtesy Shelly Parsons

91.) Ernie Hatfield at the piano, 1957.

92.) Harold Redman – drums, Stan Payne – clarinet, and Ernie Hatfield at Coe's Tavern, 1957. Both photos courtesy of Ernie Hatfield.

Floyd Standifer was fairly typical of the younger 493 Union members. Shown opposite in a later photograph, the much-beloved Seattle trumpeter and teacher was both proud of Local 493 and somewhat ambivalent about its role. Still, Standifer championed The Blue Note, stating,

> *"...One thing about the black musicians in 493, the officers were all working people – not just administrators but people who played. That engenders a certain amount of respect and regard... Guys you played with were the guys who kept the books. John Willis [493's Secretary Treasurer] was an alto player."*

Standifer noted the contrast with Local 76 officials and their policies saying, "You had to walk uphill to get in there, there'd been so much swept under the rug." Another difference for the trumpeter was a "Rainbow Coalition" atmosphere at The Blue Note. Recorded 493 members included Anglo musicians Bill Rinaldi, Traff Hubert, Mike DeFillipis, Fred Greenwell, Jan Skugstad, and Kenny Boas, as well as the Hawaiian-surnamed Edmond Kamai and Olino Kaulili, and Hispanic-surnamed Elsie Martinez.

But at the end of the day, Standifer saw the major distinction between Seattle's white and black music unions more about the actual music. Standifer was caustic about white 76 administrators who "didn't give a shit about bebop... Didn't care about the guys playin' it. They felt we were playin' wrong notes and were marginal musicians."

93.) Floyd Standifer in Seattle, July 1983.
Photo by Mary Randlett.

Among the venues which kept Seattle's jazz torch burning during the late 1950s was Pete's Poop-Deck. Here an advertisement extols the club's music policy in period parlance and graphics. The room was located then in a decidedly unhip neighborhood at 77 Main Street. Yet club owner, Pete Barbas, only 20 when he opened the room in late 1957, successfully cultivated a beat feeling and an authentic jazz policy. In the accompanying photograph, veteran 493 member Jabo Ward, who played the room for three years from 1958-1961, switches to alto from his normal tenor saxophone. Fruit crates upon which patrons also sat, double for a music stand in this "live" shot from 1959. Ward praised Barbas and his music policy stating,

> *"Pete didn't care what you played as long as it was jazz. And everybody that came there – that's what they wanted to hear was jazz. And the place stayed packed."*

Next. as this 1962 ad suggests, The Penthouse was another good bet for jazz. Particularly for name bands, it was a major Emerald City venue from 1962-1968. Charlie Puzzo ran the place, located at First Avenue and Cherry in Pioneer Square. By all accounts a modern and attractive club, it was just across the street from where Al Pierre's 1940s night spot, the Union Club originally stood. When the room opened in the 1960s the house rhythm section was Chuck Metcalf, Bill Richardson, and Dick Palumbi on bass, drums, and piano respectively. Additionally, the nightclub is immortalized as the home for John Coltrane's *Live in Seattle,* 1965 Impulse recording.

94.) Ad for Pete's Poop-Deck, c. 1962. Courtesy Ben Laigo.

95.) Jabo Ward takes charge at Pete's Poop-Deck, with Al Turay on guitar and Kenny Greig on bass, 1959. From *Seattle Post-Intelligencer* Collection, courtesy Museum of History & Industry.

96.) Diz, Ernestine, and Miles at The Penthouse, circa 1962. Courtesy Ben Laigo.

Another glimmer in a fading jazz scene of the late 1950s following the merger of Seattle's music unions is shown in these photographs. This was a coffee house, which doubled as a late-night music spot, called The Door, located at 1818 Seventh Avenue, "a block and a half away from Frederick & Nelson." It stayed open until 3:00 a.m. and was run by brothers Ben and Ed Laigo. The room featured area jazz musicians like Local 493's Elmer Gill, along with Bud Schultz, and Jerry Gray. The Door provided good music and strong coffee and displayed modern art on its walls. In an indication of tough times to come though, Ben Laigo hired swing-era violin legend Joe Venuti, then a Seattle resident. Venuti played for the lunch shift, but crowds failed to materialize and a broken-hearted, Laigo had to let the master go.

Ben Laigo was a Seattle native of Filipino ancestry who had a strong jazz background. He remembered good times in the late 1940s and early 1950s when he and his older brothers helped manage The Snack Bar on 24th and Union. There "the older type musicians like Pops Buford, Winfield King, and Terry Cruise," 493 men all, came through regularly. Laigo saw the young Quincy Jones around this time playing in a band at the Maryknoll. Laigo also fondly recalled getting into Norm Bobrow's supper club, The Colony, around 1955, when he was clearly underaged. Another memorable experience for the promoter came about during this time at Seattle University. There he got an opportunity to work with alto saxophonist and arranger Earl Bostic, then riding a wave of international success. In 1961 and 1962 Laigo branched out from his business at The Door and produced two critically well-received, but financially challenged "Aqua Jazz Concerts," at Green Lake. Due to their financial setbacks, he decided against any further large-scale jazz productions explaining,

> "The first year was all local. The second year was local, but also featured Dave Brubeck, which was a lot of money. Unfortunately, we didn't get the press we needed and got rain to boot. So, we took a beating."

97.) Ben & Ed Laigo at the register.

98.) A jam session at The Door.

99.) Bud Schultz Trio at the Door. L-R Schultz, Dan Richardson, and Joe Larson.
Photos on this page circa 1959 courtesy of Ben Laigo.

For another Seattle Filipino-American, the late 1950s were a decidedly strange time to be a union musician. Don Osias grew up in the music scene playing piano with his father Frank and others at places like the Eastside Hall, which became Birdland. Don watched clubs change and clientele come and go. Playing jazz, blues, and bump-and-grind music for strippers, he'd already been working for several years before deciding to go to one of the West Coast's premier music schools, the Westlake Music College in Los Angeles. There he studied music theory and came home in 1957 with a powerful desire to join his boyhood friend, saxophonist, combo leader, and 493 man Frank Roberts, (see accompanying photos.) Osias was set to join AFM Local 493 but was too late due to the merger. So the pianist joined 76, unlike his non-union dad Frank, but missed out on the camaraderie and only recalls one referral from Winfield King to play a gay bar, as far as any economic benefits following the amalgamation.

But the work with Roberts panned out and the piano man began playing at Dave's Fifth Avenue. As Osias recalled, the quartet was playing in a hard-edged style performing songs like "Emanon" and "Jordu," while the crowd wanted to hear "more of a commercial kind of jazz." The piano man continued to gig around town, honing his skills. But before he eventually went on to make a good living playing commercial music touring hotel chains and playing behind strippers, Osias toured with the Frank Roberts Quartet, which also included another 493 alum, drummer Dallas Schachere. The affable Osias recalled a 1959 incident on the northern "Chitlin Circuit" in Great Falls, Montana at an integrated venue known as The Ozark Club. The proprietor was Bob Mabane, who'd played tenor sax in Jay McShann's big band from 1940-1944, including the period in 1942 when Charles "Yardbird" Parker graced the reeds section. At The Ozark, Osias and the quartet gigged six days a week from September 12 through December 19 of 1959.

"We were beboppers and were in Montana. We thought we'd gone to a cowboy town – Great Falls, Montana. And we were the hip ones y'know? Young. We hit that town and – it was a gangster town. The gangsters would pull jobs on the East Coast and come to Great Falls to cool off. What do they call it, 'whack' somebody? The dude used to come over. I'd be rehearsing at the club during the day, and the dude was a whacker – one of the executioners. In 1959 he drove a '60 Cadillac. And he'd throw a bag of weed on the keyboards and say, 'Roll me up some and take some for yourself.'... They're nice guys. If you're on their side (laughs.)".

100.) Frank Roberts Trio. L-R: Don Osias, piano; Jay Jasane, drums; and Frank Roberts, baritone saxophone, c. 1957.

101.) Frank Roberts Quartet, Ozark Club Great Falls, Montana, September 1959. L-R back row: Don Osias, piano; Dallas Schachere, drums. Front row: Charles B., – tenor saxophone; and Frank Roberts – baritone sax.

Both photos courtesy Don Osias.

That same year in 1959 gave three other members of Seattle's black musicians' union a chance for international recognition, as can be seen in the accompanying photograph. Having left Seattle, Quincy Delight Jones was then living in Paris. Through music impresario John Hammond, Jones met Stanley Chase, a producer of a Harold Arlen/Johnny Mercer show for which Quincy was to provide a dream band. Set for a four city European run, the show was to then go on to London, and finally to Broadway in New York. However, things did not go as planned.

One year after Local 493 had merged with its white counterpart, Jones headed up an all-star band with the likes of Clark Terry, Budd Johnson, Melba Liston, Benny Bailey, and Phil Woods. But Q didn't forget "my homeys from Seattle," and hired three African American musicians who'd all belonged to 493. In this photograph Seattle pianist Patti Bown is second from right, eighth from right Buddy Catlett holds his bass bow, while Floyd Standifer sits with trumpet on the far left in the first row. They were all part of the orchestra for the play *Free and Easy*. But after two months of rehearsing in Holland, the show ran for just six weeks in Paris. When the production folded, Quincy, noting that this was "the best band I ever had," reached into his own pocket to keep the big band together. Travelling through Europe "like vagabonds" on the strength of the well-received, Birth of a Band album, it was a rollercoaster of a tour. At one point the 26 year-old Jones was paid off in Yugoslavian currency – worthless in the West. So, he gambled on the rest of an unbooked tour itinerary and spent the equivalent of $62,000 in Yugoslav Dinars on train tickets. A few good breaks and a lot of love kept the band in Europe for another 10 months, although Jones returned to the United States "dead broke and deeply in debt." Despite considerable hard times, Quincy saw fit to praise all the members of the band later in his 2001 autobiography. And it is noteworthy that the entire big band stayed with him for the full tour. Here they are immortalized on stage at the Paris Alhambra Theatre Music Hall.

102.) The Quincy Jones Big Band, on stage at the Paris Alhambra, 1959 in the blues opera, Free and Easy. Back Row L-R: Budd Johnson, clarinet; Patti Bown, piano; Lennie Johnson, trumpet; Julius Watkins, French horn; Jerome Richardson, flute; Les Spann, flute; Aake Persson, trombone; Buddy Catlett, bass; Clark Terry, trumpet; Quentin Jackson, trombone; Jimmy Cleveland, trombone; Benny Bailey, trumpet; and Melba Liston, trombone. Front row: Floyd Standifer, trumpet; Sahib Shihab, flute; Porter Kilbert, alto saxophone; Joe Harris, drums; Quincy Jones, leader; and Phil Woods, alto sax. Photo courtesy of Lola Pedrini.

For the second to the last photograph in this history, it is appropriate to salute a fellow traveler with the 493 men and women. A grandson of early jazz legend Edythe Turnham, Al Hilbert was one of those who capitalized on Seattle's famed "tolerance policy" and helped shape it into a decidedly sophisticated and pleasurable experience. This free-wheeling climate continued full bore until at least 1949 when the Washington State Legislature eventually made it legal to serve hard liquor by the drink. Such a wide-open atmosphere created its own demi-monde where an alternate life of drinking, dining, dancing, jazz music, gambling, and other pastimes all flourished in a decidedly convivial manner. Or in Viola Howell's apt phrase, "If you had money you were tolerated."

Barkeep Hilbert smiles while serving customers at the old Ebony Club. Hilbert, who made a good living managing rooms and gambling concessions during the 1940s boom years, was also connected to Seattle's jazz world (see page 141.) Going back to 1929, as a youngster he drove his grandmother and early 493 unionist Edythe Turnham and her Black Hawks big band all over downtown Seattle. Barnstorming the city, as she and her band played from the back of a flatbed truck, he helped publicize Ms. Turnham's shows. As Hilbert's wan smile suggests, he knew how to let the good times roll. This situation at the Ebony Club and many other venues of the day coexisted side-by-side with jazz played by a small group of musicians, most of whom were union members of Local 493.

103.) Tolerance Personified – Al Hilbert serves a round to (L-R) Duke Dupree and Phil Burton, circa 1949-1950 at the Ebony Club. Photo courtesy Dorothy Hilbert.

The curtain closer on this history of race, music, and unionism is dedicated to Mr. Powell Barnett. This tuba player and tireless political organizer was one of the chief architects of first Local 458, then Local 493 and by extension its famous clubhouse Local, The Blue Note. Perhaps no other figure is quite so central to this story. To be sure no one else was a lifetime member of both the black *and* white musicians' unions. In 1918 at the beginning, Powell Barnett was one of the founders of the "Colored Musicians' Union, Local 458," which somewhat fitfully, yet effectively helped black musicians negotiate Jim Crow Seattle work rules until April of 1924. This is after Barnett had already joined white Local 76 in 1913 and made an initial attempt then to bring in other African American musicians into the mother Local.

Again, Powell Barnett's name appears prominently in behind-the-scenes actions, which set the stage for the birth of Local 493 in December of 1924. This was the black musicians' union which, unlike Los Angeles, Chicago, and other segregated black unions, welcomed Hawaiian and Hispanic-surnamed members, as well as hip, white swing and bop musicians. Barnett also figures in the final amalgamation negotiations with Local 76 in January of 1958, as a key intermediary for white 76 officials. Remaining a union man his entire life, Barnett's golden "Life Member" card is shown here. It was awarded to the dual unionist on January 10, 1951 by then "white" Local 76, while Barnett was still active in Local 493.

104.) Powell Barnett's Lifetime Membership Card from A.F. of M. Local 76, 1951.
Image courtesy of Helen and James Smith.

Appendix

The following three pages provide the only known list of the members of the Musicians' Association Local 493 American Federation of Musicians. This document is annotated as the "New Members From Amalgamation with Local 493." Dated January 14, 1958, it was the time of the final merger of the black union with white Local 76. During this historic event there were 101 dues-paying 493 members, who became "New Members" in the previously white Local 76. As a primary source it is appropriate to include the list here in tribute to those undersung, working musicians whose names may now be obscured by time.

105.) Local 493 Membership List, page 1. Courtesy A. F. of M. Local 76-493.

(2) Cont

Name	Address	City	Phone	Soc. Sec. N	Birthdate	Date of Joining Local 493	Age at Time of Joining 493	Instrument Played	Initiation Fee	Amount Paid or for Year
GUY, EDWARD	7104 Nury Hong Dr	Seattle			3-13-34	May -56	26	Bass Viol	50⁰⁰	
HALL, O'DELL	2303 E. Columbia	Seattle	CA 3184		8-12-12	9-15-55		Drums	50⁰⁰ 70 9/5	10⁰⁰
HARRISON, ZACKEL	2208 E. Terrace	Seattle	FR 6194			5-10-43 14	34	Trumpet	50⁰⁰ 5⁰⁰	15⁰⁰
HATFIELD, ERNEST J.	2811 Harrison	Seattle	EA 4658		7-5-14	1-2-53 5	39	Piano	50⁰⁰ 5⁰⁰	15⁰⁰
HILLIARD, BARNEY	2311 E. Roy	Seattle	MI 7065		1-06-37	8-3-54 3	17	Tenor Sax	50⁰⁰ 5⁰⁰	15⁰⁰
HOLDEN, DAVE	2017 Dearborn	Seattle	FR 5761		5-24-37	5-3-56 1	19	Piano	50⁰⁰	
HOLDEN, OSCAR	1409 E. Fir	Seattle	CA 4815		1-18-87	July -40 19	43	Piano	50⁰⁰ 5⁰⁰	15⁰⁰
JOHNSON, WILLIAM A.	347 25th. Ave.	Seattle	FR 3318		1-10-31	5-10-48 9	17	Drums - Bass Viol	50⁰⁰ 5⁰⁰	15⁰⁰
JONES, LASAUL	609 27th No. 2411 E.	Seattle	EA 0352		11-04-37	11-9-51 6	14	Bass Viol		
JONES, RUSSELL L.	12 N.E. Fremont	Portland			7-17-06	4-5-52 5	46	Drums & Vocals		500
JONES, DERNIECE H. (MELODY)	2904 E. Howell	Seattle	EA 1968		2-28-06	11-27-51 5	41	Piano - Hise & Ex. Organ	50⁰⁰	15⁰⁰
JOSEPH, WILLIAM	1911½ E. Thomas	Seattle	EA 1079		11-22-08	10-44 18	36	Alto Sax & Clar	50⁰⁰ 5⁰⁰	15⁰⁰
KING, WINFIELD	2415 E. Prospect	Seattle	FR 1979		2-13-30	3-3-47 10	17	Piano & Vocal		
KNOX, FRED D.	1412 23rd. Ave.	Seattle	CA 9656		4-8-33	8-11-59	24	Vibes, Xylophone & Marimba	50⁰⁰	
LARKINS, ALVIN W.	818 30th. Ave.	Seattle	FR 0962		7-15-24	1-15-46 11	21	Tuba & Bass Viol	50⁰⁰ 5⁰⁰	15⁰⁰
LEWIS, DAVID	100 100th. No.	Seattle	FR 7554		8-6-38	8-4-54 3	16	Piano	50⁰⁰ 5⁰⁰	15⁰⁰
LEWIS, EMMETT	2805 E. Spring	Seattle	CA 8093		11-15-10	11-15-45 12	34	Drums	50⁰⁰ 5⁰⁰	15⁰⁰
LEWIS, JOHN L.	824 29th. Ave.	Seattle	MI 3823		2-23-34	June -56 1	21		50⁰⁰	
LOWELL, DANIEL J.	9256 47th. S.W.	Seattle	AV 2470		8-13-40	11-28-57 8	17	Piano, Trumpet & Fr. Horn	50⁰⁰	
MARTINEZ, ELSIE (LANE)	7521 Empire Way	Seattle			1-29-13	4-29-55	42	Piano & Hise Organ	50⁰⁰ 70 9/3	10⁰⁰
MCLEAN, ALFRED SCOTT	1440 El Camino Rd.	Burlingame Calif.			4-04-29	3-17-52 5	23	Drums	50⁰⁰	
MC KEE, GOSSIE D.	8501 Sunset Blvd.	W. Los Angeles				6-21-48		Guitar	50⁰⁰	
MONTGOMERY, CHARLES	% Jazz Showcase	San. Fran. 90 Market St				1-12-59		Vibes	50⁰⁰	
MONTGOMERY, WM. H.	% Jazz Showcase	San. Fran. 90 Market St.			2-10-21	10-1-56 1	35	Bass Viol	50⁰⁰	
MOOREHEAD, MIKE E.	817 32nd. South	Seattle	MI 5947		9-19-13	1-2-54	40	Piano	50⁰⁰ 70 9/3	
MARSHALL, ROBERT	331 30th. Ave.	Seattle	EA 0749		3-25-14	4-6-45 10	31	Bass Viol	50⁰⁰ 5⁰⁰	15⁰⁰
MOTON, JOHN	900 26th. Ave.	Seattle	FR 5054		11-10-30	4-28-50	20	Piano - Vocal & Arranger	50⁰⁰	15⁰⁰
MOORE, WM "DUKE"	% Noahs Tavern				9-19-23	1-2-53 5	29	Drums	50⁰⁰	
PAYNE, STANLEY	951 21st. Ave	Seattle	MI 1998		11-4-11	7-15-45 14	33	Tenor Sax & Clarinet	50⁰⁰ 5⁰⁰	15⁰⁰
PHILLIPS, BERTRAND	952 20th. Ave.	Seattle	RA 0740		6-4-17	4-10-52 5	34	Baritone Sax & Clarinet	50⁰⁰	15⁰⁰
PITTMAN, MARK	6828 Holly Park	Seattle	MO 2243		9-4-10	3-15-45 5	34	Bass Viol & Bass Horn	50⁰⁰	15⁰⁰
PORTER, EVAN	1607½ E. Columbia	Seattle	EA 6739		3-12-28	2-15-55	26	Trumpet & Piano	50⁰⁰	15⁰⁰
PRITCHARD, EARL O.	128 24th. No.	Seattle	EA 3851		10-27-15	5-14-55	39	Drums & Percussions Tymps Etc.	50⁰⁰	15⁰⁰
RICHARDSON, WILLARD V	510 33rd. Ave.	Seattle	CA 8385		5-10	8-11-49 8	41	Piano	50⁰⁰ 5⁰⁰	
RICHARDSON, WILLIAM	3005 E. Union	Seattle	MI 9147		7-16-27	4-1-59 10	30	Drums	50⁰⁰	
ROBINSON, RAY CHAS.	% Shaw Artists Corp	New York	(565 Fifth)			1- -54		Piano & Vocal		
ROARK, EDWARD I	14850 5th. N.E.	Seattle	GL 3136		9-4-37	11-20-57 8	20	Piano, Bass Viol, Saxophones	50⁰⁰	
ROBERTS, ALEXANDER F		SEATTLE	MI 7639		4-7-34	2-24-53 4	18	Baritone Sax & Clar	50⁰⁰ 5⁰⁰	15⁰⁰
RUSSELL, ROBERT L.	138 30th. Ave.	Seattle	EA 6407		8-28-09	5-14-45	36	Trumpet - Valve Trombone, Drums	50⁰⁰ 5⁰⁰	15⁰⁰

106.) Local 493 Membership List, page 2. Courtesy A. F. of M. Local 76-493.

107.) Local 493 Membership List, page 3. Courtesy A. F. of M. Local 76-493.

Notes

1.) "Interview 6 February 1962," Powell Barnett Manuscripts; Author Interview Douglas Q. Barnett; *Spawn of Coal Dust: History of Roslyn, 1886-1955*; and Charles Lovell, *Through Open Eyes*. Roslyn founded in 1886 by Logan M. Bullett, vice president of the Northern Pacific Coal Co. In 1888 the Knights of Labor began a strike, which brought black miners to the region. See *Through Open Eyes*; and Tom Hackenmiller, *Labor Unions in the Upper Kittitas County*, 13-15; and "Roslyn Black Mining Family," circa 1890 photographs 1-8, *Roslyn Black History*, Ellensburg Public Library. Population of Roslyn in 1900 was 2,786 with 317 black residents, *Roslyn Black History*, 13. American Federation of Miners in Roslyn 1904, from *The Cascade Miner*, 24 October 1908, and from *Spawn*, 209. AFM Local 76 Monthly Meeting Minutes (MMM) 9 August 1918.

2.) Douglas Q. Barnett Interview; "Interview 6 February 1962," Powell Barnett Manuscripts, 6; and *The Seattle Medium*, 14 February 1974, 13.

3.) Powell Barnett Manuscripts, 7-9. Earlier bands in "Roslyn Lodge Parade, 1899," 4-8, in *Roslyn Black History*, 18.

4.) Lacy's Band in Paul de Barros, *Jackson Street After Hours: The Roots of Jazz in Seattle*, 7. Population growth in Richard C. Berner, *Seattle 1921-1940: From Boom To Bust*, 214; and Quintard Taylor, *The Forging Of A Black Community: Seattle's Central District from 1870 through the Civil Rights Era*, 52.

5.) Powell Barnett Manuscripts, 19-20 and in Powell Barnett Manuscripts, "Volunteers of America Interview." Tenth Division Band references throughout Barnett Manuscripts, particularly, "Organizations," 2; and in Robert Bradford Pitts, "Organized Labor and the Negro in Seattle," 67. Parks' performances in "Organized Labor and the Negro," and Author Interview James T. "Smitty" Smith, 10 March 2000. Barnett breaks color bar in Local 76 Board Meeting Minutes (BMM) 21, 28 May 1913, and 31 December 1913. Birth of Local 458 in MMM 9 August 1918, MMM 20 August 1918, and BMM 3 September 1918.

6.) Whang Doodle Orchestra labeled as a "colored quartet" for an infraction in BMM 17 December 1918. Local 76's Sergeant at Arms charges that only one band member is a dues paying union member but continues that Local 458 had the matter "straightened up to the satisfaction of this local" in BMM 23 December 1918. Waldron's influence in *Jackson Street*.

7.) Phil Pastras, *Dead Man Blues: Jelly Roll Morton Way Out West*, 33, 42-43, 75, 91-114. Also in *Jackson Street*, pp. 1, 11, 213. Pastras refers to Jerome Pasqual's quote placing Jelly in Seattle in June of 1920, on which de Barros relies heavily as a "vague reminiscence," cited in Laurie Wright, *Mr. Jelly Lord*, p. 4, in *Dead Man*, 221. See also The West Coast Years in Lawrence Gushee, "A Preliminary Chronology of the Early Career of Ferdinand 'Jelly Roll' Morton," 1985, *American Music*, 405-408. Holden's daughter, Grace, maintains that Morton worked for Holden. See Kurt E. Armbruster's *Before Seattle Rocked: A City and Its Music*, 341. Morton's vaudeville background in "A Preliminary Chronology," 400-403. Morton's work in various areas in Alan Lomax's *Mister Jelly Roll*, 22-145. Gushee citation establishes

Morton as a Vancouver, B.C. Local 145 member and playing with Local 458 men and traveling members. Vancouver sidemen in Mark Miller, *Jazz In Canada: Fourteen Lives,* 4, 12. Eubanks & Morton in Vancouver also in John Chilton, *Who's Who of Jazz: Storyville to Swing Street,* 106, 234. Further Morton background from Mark Cave *Jazz Scrapbook: Bill Russell and Some Highly Musical Friends,* "Jelly Roll Morton: Shoe Shiner's Drag," 17-27. Morton's version including sidemen and gambling in *Mister Jelly Roll,* 170-172. Morton's copyrighting style in *Dead Man,* 139.

8.) Apology letter in BMM 25 February 1924. Female membership in *International Musician (IM),* May 1921, 25, BMM 26 February 1924. Mrs. Austin as Secretary in BMM 1 December 1931. Gertrude Wright details from March 24, 2009 and Jacqueline E.A. Lawson email. See also David Keller, "Sweethearts of Jazz: The Women of Seattle's Black Musicians' Unions," *Columbia* Magazine, Winter 2009-10. For slightly different treatment see Keller's "Race, Gender, Jazz, & Local 493: Black Women Musicians in Seattle, 1920-1955," *BlackPast.org,* 18 July 2010. More in Quintard Taylor, *In Search of the Racial Frontier,* 250, and *Jackson Street,* 20-26. Intra-union charges detailed in BMM 27 December 1923, 15 January 1924, 5 and 19 February 1924. Charges and charter revocation in BMM 11 & 19 March, 15 & 22 April, 20 May 1924. Union membership in "Organized Labor and the Negro," 70-71.

9.) *Musicland* 15 June 1922. See also Eleanor Siegl, "The Amalgamation of the Colored and White Musicians' Unions in Seattle," 3; Conover, "The Good Old Days of 'Dad': Theodore Wagner's Band," *Seattle Times,* no date; and "Roslyn's Band," photo and caption in *Roslyn Black History,* 13, where the Roslyn Band won second prize against Wagner's and Sousa's Bands at the 1909 Seattle Potlatch Festival. Membership in "Organized Labor and the Negro," 67, 71. "Maniacs" story in *Musicland* 5 January 1922. Black bourgeois response in *Cayton's Monthly,* February 1920, 10. Thanks to Rick Hobbs for citation. Fictive treatment in "Mumbo Jumbo" in *The Reed Reader,* Ishmael Reed, 31-57. Leonard Gayton in *Jackson Street,* 22. Later anti-jazz bill covered in Peter Blecha's "'Jazz Intoxication' bill is introduced in Washington State Legislature on December 22, 1933," http://www.historylink.org.

10-11.) Turnham Spokane residence and marriage from Washington State Digital Archives, http://www.digitalarchives.wa.gov and 1907-1919 Spokane City directories. Thanks to Spokane Northwest Room Librarian Riva Dean for this lead, and to Jacqueline E.A. Lawson for further Spokane and age confirmations in 1910 Federal Census. More in *Jackson Street,* 7, 24, 25, 28. See BMM 10 August 1926 re: Black Satin Orchestra and BMM 8 November 1927 for day off dispute. Ad in *Musicland* 25 August 1928. More in BMM July 25, 1928 and August 10, 1928. Plantation flyer from Washington State Historical Society, #1994.1.3.62 on page 8 of "Sweethearts of Jazz." See also "Race, Gender, Jazz, & Local 493." Floyd Jr., and Club Alabam in Frank Driggs and Harris Lewine, *Black Beauty, White Heat: A Pictorial History of Classic Jazz, 1920-1950,* 188.

12.) Nanking Restaurant, Frank Waldron, and Odean Jazz Orchestra in *Jackson Street,* 5-7, 213, 221. Publishing and school account in Merle Irene Smith, *Seattle Had a Tin Pan Alley, Too! 7,* 47. Violation of 7-day work rule by Nanking Orchestra in BMM 29 September 1925 and BMM 6 October 1925.

13.) Ad & Valhalla listing from unattributed newspaper clippings Mary E. Adams Collection. See also *Forging,* 149, and *Jackson Street,* 20, 39. Shanghai Restaurant and 493 member dispute in BMM 27 March 1928.

14.) *Jackson Street,* 17, 3, 30. See also Daphne Duval Harrison, *Black Pearls: Blues Queens of the 1920s,* 40–42, 45–48; Orrin Keepnews and Bill Grauer, Jr. *A Pictorial History of Jazz: People and Places From*

New Orleans to the Sixties, 72; Leonard Feather, *The Encyclopedia of Jazz,* 422-423; and Eileen Southern, *The Music of Black Americans: A History,* 397-398. Smith backed by white band in Ed Kirkeby, *Ain't Misbehavin': The Story of Fats Waller,* 65-66. William Howland Kenney in *Recorded Music In American Life,* 114, contradicts this, stating that Smith was backed by her black band, The Jazz Hounds. However, Kirkeby supplies more detail for the white band of Frederick Wallace Hager, who used the song-writing synonym of Wallace Rega. Additionally, Kirkeby explained that composer Perry Bradford maintained that Smith was backed for this session by "an ofay band, (the Rega Orchestra.)" More sales and record background in *Who's Who of Jazz, 305;* and Mary Schmidt Campbell, David Driskell, David Levering, Deborah Lewis Ryan, *Harlem Renaissance: Art of Black America,* 169. Hawkins and West Coast tour from Kenny Berger, "Coleman Hawkins," in *The Oxford Companion to Jazz,* 180. While Bradford made money on composer royalties, this was an exception and many black artists were forced to sign away their rights. See *Recorded Music,* 127-128.

15.) *Jackson Street,* 17, although no other corroboration could be found for Bessie Smith's appearance in Seattle. Recording background from Bill Wyman with Richard Havers, *Bill Wyman's Blues Odyssey: A Journey to Music's Heart and Soul,* 80-81. Edison in Brian Robertson, *Little Blues Book,* 81. More in Chris Albertson, "Bessie Smith," 78-79, 83-87 in *Oxford Companion.* See also Chris Albertson *Bessie; Black Pearls,* 51-52; and *Music of Black Americans,* 398-399. Music on film in Meeker, *Jazz In The Movies,* Numbers 722, 1287, 491, and 2276, and "St. Louis Blues" in http://video.yahoo.com/watch/634140/298693, solo discography https://syncopatedtimes.com/bessie-smith-1895-1937/. Peabody detail from "Eddie Peabody 1902-1970," by Sean Moyses, https://syncopatedtimes.com/eddie-peabody-1902-1970/l.

16.) Ad in holiday issue of *Musicland* December 1927, 2. Background and Bellingham information from Author Interviews Roy Green, 5 March 1996, and Dan Mather, 20 November 2000. More in "Eddie Peabody 1902-1970." Performance style from "The Hal Kemp Band with Eddie Peabody," 1928, and "Painting the Clouds With Sunshine," 1929, www.youtube.com. On the power of the phonograph see *Recorded Music,* and the more specialized, *Jazz on Record: A History* by Brian Priestley. Fifth Avenue show in *Musicland,* 10 April 1928, 4.

17.) Photo from unattributed clipping Burnett Collection. Whiteman background in Gary Giddins, *Bing Crosby: A Pocketful of Dreams: The Early Years 190 -1940,* 141-159, 160-185, and Gunther Schuller, *Early Jazz: Its Roots and Musical Development,* 192. For jazz in white market see Richard Sudhalter, *Lost Chords: White Musicians and Their Contribution to Jazz, 1915-1945,* 14-17, 37-38, 52-58, 103-104, 136-137, 159-180, Sudhalter liner notes in *The Jazz Age.* "Whispering" and "Rhapsody in Blue" details in *Recorded Music,* 63, and in William Howland Kenney, *Chicago Jazz: A Cultural History, 1904-1930,* 78-79. Still and KFI from "William Grant Still Dean of Afro-American Composers," by Catherine Parsons Smith, 44, in *Music In The Central Avenue Community 1890-c.1955.* Venuti quote and time with Whiteman from Ian Carr, Digby Fairweather and Brian Priestley, *Jazz: The Rough Guide,* 662. Venuti and Seattle in *Jackson Street,* 199. Crosby and Renker in band from *Bing Crosby,* 160-185, and *Jackson Street,* 35. Burnett background in *Seattle Post-Intelligencer,* 2 May 1964; "Melody Lingers On," Don Duncan, "Last Attraction: 'Death of the Orpheum,'" *Seattle Times,* no date; and *Seattle Times,* 24 March, 1917. Membership in *Jackson Street,* 33. Bruce Lawrence from Douglas Barnett letter to author 31 May 2002 and Paul de Barros *Seattle Times,* 30 May 2002, "One Symphony Musician Grew Up Playing with Harlem's Greats."

18-19.) Clip in *Musicland,* December 1927 and Author's collection. Brunswick Orchestra in *Seattle*

Had A Tin Pan Alley, Too!, 57, 63. Herb Wiedoeft details from www.parabrisas.com/d_wiedoefth.php and www.search.com/reference/Rudy_Wiedoeft. Discography in https://web.archive.org/web/20170709165555fw_/http://redhotjazz.com/wiedoefto.html. More in *Jackson Street*, 52. Racially segregated audience from Kenney, *Recorded Music,* 62. Radio station management meetings in BMM, 29 September 1925.

20.) "Vic and the Boys" in *Musicland* 20 November 1926, 5, with earliest photo ad in *Musicland*, 15 June 1923 through December 1928 in Holiday Issue. Song and additional details from *Seattle Had A Tin Pan Alley, Too!,* 63. Brunswick recording from Meyers cassette tape provided to author by Dan Mather 6 August 1994. Columbia recording from author's collection. More in *Jackson Street,* 33-35. Butler Hotel staff and turf fight from Esther Mumford, "Charles Lewis Interview," 27 August 1975. 3, 15.

21.) Black and Tan definition from Author Interview, Floyd Standifer, 16 January 1996. Ellington phrase in Krin Gabbard, *Jammin' At the Margins: Jazz and the American Cinema*, 64. Alhambra from *Jackson Street*, 3. More in 7 August 1946 *Northwest Enterprise (NWE)*. Other acts in *NWE,* 18 November 1938, 7 June 1944, and 14 August 1950. Robert Wright as nephew of Noodles Smith from Jacqueline E.A. Lawson. Al Smith quote from Author Interview 30 June 2000. Smith worked as a Seattle club photographer from the 1920s through the 1980s, chronicling both musicians and fans activities with his Speed Graphic large format camera. The backs of his photographs were stamped with his trademark, "Al Smith on the spot." More about Smith from *"Jazz on the Spot*: The Photography of Al Smith," Museum of History and Industry (MOHAI) exhibit, curated by Paul de Barros and Howard Giske, October 15, 1993 - January 31, 1994, and Charles E. Brown, "Al Smith Sr., Photographer, Historian" in *Seattle Times*, 5 September 2008. More in *Forging*, 147. See also the "Battle Royal" in *NE, 14 September 1933.*

22.) Radio management meetings in BMM 29 September 1925. Early broadcasts from Author Interview Floyd Standifer. Fatha Hines and Grand Terrace NBC shows from Stanley Dance, *The World of Earl Hines*, 63. KOL & KXA broadcasts in Joe Darensbourg with Peter Vacher, *A Jazz Odyssey: The Autobiography of Joe Darensbourg,* 75, 77, 90. KJR live shows in Fred Cordova, *Filipinos, Forgotten Asian Americans: A Pictorial Essay 1763- circa 1963*, 88-90. Armstrong on radio station WSMB in *Black Beauty,* 30, Gary Giddins, *Satchmo*, 113-115, and Nat Hentoff, *Jazz Is*, 72-73. Pop's last laugh in Thomas Brothers, editor, *Louis Armstrong, In His Own Words,* 145, 147.

23.) 1932 A. F. of M. meeting in Powell Barnett Manuscripts, "Musicians' Convention L. A. –1933 (sic)." Also, in Local 76-493 working file, "Powell Barnett," no date at Local 76-493 Union Headquarters Seattle; and in *Jackson Street*, 97, 102, and Author Interview Standifer. For comparisons with San Francisco and an excellent overview of national merger policies see Leta E. Miller, "Racial Segregation and the San Francisco Musicians' Union, 1923-60," *Journal of the Society for American Music,* 161-206. Also in *Jackson Street Community Council Newsletter,* 15 October 1963. Barnett's resolve may have been strengthened in this matter since at least one interracial band existed in Seattle at this time. In 1930-1932 white bassist and guitar man Bill Rinaldi worked with self-described New Orleans, "Creole" saxophonist Joe Darensbourg in The Genessee Street Shufflers. See *Jazz Odyssey*, 81 and *Jackson Street*, 21, 38. The Shufflers featured white pianist Vic Sewell, who lived on Genesee Street, and white drummer Jack Foy. This racially mixed Seattle band precedes national trends by four years, when Benny Goodman hired Teddy Wilson and Lionel Hampton in 1936. See Charley Gerard, *Jazz in Black and White: Race, Culture, and Identity in the Jazz Community,* 20-23. Rinaldi probably joined Local 493 around this time and is definitely a member of "the colored musicians' union" by March 30, 1937 when he is identified as such in a Special Meeting of the Executive Board (SMEB) by Local 76.

24.) Coy background in Ross Russell, *Jazz Style in Kansas City and the Southwest*, 58-59; *Handbook of Texas Online*, bio by Dave Oliphant, in http://www.tsha.utexas.edu/handbook/online/articles/CC/fcods.html, and in NFO.NET *Big Bands Database Plus* by Dan Del Fiornetino in http://info.net/usa/cf/html. Webster with Coy for nine months beginning in 1929 in Les Tomkins "Jazz Professional Ben Webster Talking to Les Tomkins in 1965," www.jazzprofessional.com/interviews/BenWebster.htm, 1. More on Webster in John Chilton, *Who's Who*, 345. See also Gunther Schuller, *The Swing Era: The Development of Jazz, 1930-1945*, 285; See also *Jazz Odyssey*, 75 re: Coy at Butler Hotel. More on Coy in *Jackson Street*, 39-42. Aces in Grand Coulee and Junior Raglin information from *IM*, January 1939, Vol. 37, page 18. Author Interview Al Turay 20 April 2001, and Scott DeVeaux, *The Birth of Bebop: A Social and Musical History*, p. 196. Howard McGee quote in *Birth of Bebop*, 196. Dick Wilson, Durham brothers, Ewing, Byers, and other LA musicians with Coy from Peter Vacher's *Swingin' on Central Avenue*, 107, 110, 112, 240-242. Special thanks to Peter for this tip and the uncirculated photo. Robert Wright in *Forging*, 147.

25.) Julius Mattfeld, *Variety Music Cavalcade*, 378.

26.) "Gray area" from Author Interview, Don Osias, 30 March 2000. Additional research in Local 76-493 records, *Musicland* and *International Musician* produced no listings for any Filipino-surnamed musicians. Rizal bio from William H. Harris and Judith S. Levey, *The New Columbia Encyclopedia*, 2331. Fictional account of the Rizal and Seattle's International District underworld in Carlos Bulosan, *America Is In The Heart*, 104-106. Song repertoire from Author Interview, Frank Osias, 30 March 2000.

27.) Interracial marriage from Carey McWilliams, "Introduction," *America Is In The Heart*, vii-xxiv. Tour activity detailed in Author Interview Frank Osias.

28.) *NWE*, 17 May 1934, 1. Ertegan and Pullman details in Derek Jewell, *Duke: A Portrait of Duke Ellington*, 55, 59. See also John Edward Hasse, *Beyond Category: The Life and Genius of Duke Ellington*, 180-181. Hasse notes that the band sometimes had its own dining car as well. More in Scott Yanow, *Duke Ellington*, 46-47 and James Lincoln Collier, *Duke Ellington*, 132-133. While Irving Mills fought for dignity for his musicians, he was not above stealing from them. According to Duke's son Mercer, Mills did not write any of the Ellington lyrics he is credited with, beginning with *Ring Dem Bells* and totaling some sixty songs. In addition, he stole an estimated seventy five percent of Ellington's royalties, "the entire publisher's share and half the author's share," see *Beyond Category*, 129. Detail on Snakehips (for whom Ellington was said to have written, "The Mooche,") from Al Smith Interview. 767's Les Hite & 493 in Regular Meeting of the Associated Minutes (RMAA,) 4 June 1935. Hite Olympic Hotel performance in Regular Meeting Executive Board (RMEB) 15 January 1935. Chicago 208 members, with Nat Cole and John L. Thomas as 493 travelling members in *IM*, May 1937, Volume 35, 18. "Shuffle Along" detail in *Who's Who of Jazz*, 75, 326, and in James Haskin with Kathleen Benson, *Nat King Cole*, 21-23. 767's Les Hite band in *IM*, July 1936, Volume 34, p.7, and August 1938, Volume 37, p. 18. Hampton paying dues to Local 76 in *IM*, January 1936, Volume 33, p. 10. Ellington dues activity from *IM*, April 1937, Volume 35, p. 15. More on tour 493 dues payments in *Amalgamation of the Colored*, 4. Seattle musicians with national bands from *Jackson Street*, 85-86, 114. Interview, William Funderberg, 20 May 1996 and in RMAA, 7 July 1948. In the latter, a long-standing "controversy" involving a 1947 Ink Spots show at the Orpheum for $1312.50 paid to 76 for a minimum of 12 local men was finally successfully adjudicated with 493. See also RMBD 4, 12 and 19 June 1947.

29.) *NWE,* 15 August 1935. Hampton tour particulars in Lionel Hampton and James Haskins *Hamp: An Autobiography,* 40-42.

30.) *NWE,* 15 December 1935. Mills bookings and conditions in *Beyond Category,* 167-169, 176. Calloway background from Jim Haskins, *The Cotton Club,* pp. 63-66. Calloway recording in *Encyclopedia of Jazz,* 152. Ellington leaves Cotton Club February 2, 1931 in *Beyond Category,* 139. Cotton Club background in *The Cotton Club,* 28-79. See also *Beyond Category,* 98-116, 138-142, and Ted Gioia *The History of Jazz,* 131. More on big bands in clubs from *Forging,* 147-149, and "Charles Lewis Interview," 3. Seattle's Cotton Club in *NWE,* 22 January 1931, 6.

31.) Shanghai jazz scene from Driggs and Lewine, *Black Beauty,* 206, 209; *Jackson Street,* 47-49; Frederick Starr, *Red and Hot: The Fate of Jazz in the Soviet Union,* 226-227; George Yoshida, *Reminiscing in Swingtime,* 87; and *All About Shanghai and Environs,* 43. Johnson letter from unattributed newspaper clipping in Mary E. Adams collection. See also *Jazz Odyssey,* 75, 77. Clayton at Canindrome from *All About Shanghai,* 43, 76. Further background in Harriet Sergeant, *Shanghai: Collision Point of Cultures,* 10-67.

32.) *NWE,* 18 November 1938. Johnson description from *Jazz Odyssey,* 77, Wally Macdonald *A 49 Year Musical History of the Northwest,* 17, and "Governor's Heritage Award – Palmer Johnson," from https://www.arts.wa.gov/wp-content/uploads/2022/06/Archive-of-Honorees.pdf. Further discussion on jamming on page 88 in this work. After-hours jams in *Jackson Street,* 44. Al Turay from Author Interview. For a cultural context to jamming, although author makes no mention about A. F. of M work rules, see Peter Townsend, *Jazz in American Culture, 1918-1939,* 45-61.

33.) Wilson in Seattle from Al Smith photo data at Black Heritage Society Collection MOHAI. See also *Jackson Street,* 39-40. More in *Jazz Odyssey,* 74-75. Travel and studies in *Who's Who of Jazz,* 359. Further background in Linda Dahl, *Morning Glory: A Biography of Mary Lou Williams,* 97-98, 100; *The Swing Era,* 351-352; and *Encyclopedia, of Jazz,* 465.

34.) Men of Jazz from Jacqueline E.A. Lawson telephone interview, and Black Heritage Society Collection, MOHAI. Further background on location of clubs and halls in Jacqueline E. A. Lawson, *Let's Take A Walk: A Tour of Seattle's Central Area As It Was Then, 1920s and 1930s.* Tolles and Pigford from *Jackson Street,* 70-72. Appearance in *NWE,* 10 March 1943, 1 and Peter Blecha, "Birdland: Seattle's Fabled 1950s R&B Hotspot," 1. in https://www.historylink.org.

35.) Union history from Author Interview Standifer. Pierre background and Williams quote from Robert Dietsche, *Jumptown: The Golden Years of Portland Jazz, 1942-1957.* More in *Jackson Street,* 62-64. Jabo Ward from Author Interview 20 May 1996. More in Dorothy Hilbert Author Interview 18 February 2000. Beverly Kelly quotes from Author Interview 24 February 2000.

36.) Dorothy Lomax quote and material from Author Interview 22 March 2000. Charles and Young at Elks' Club in *Jackson Street,* 151. See also *Forging,* 139, on the importance of black benevolent organizations like the Elks' as a source of race pride, positive images and self-determination.

37-38.) African Americans and baseball in Seattle from Lyle Kenai Wilson, *Sunday Afternoon at Garfield Park*, 17-49. Barnett and community in *NE*, 23 June 1939, cited in *Sunday Afternoon*, 44. See also Kelly quote from Author Interview. Jazz and baseball from Ken Poston, "Swing Into Spring," Los Angeles Jazz Institute brochure, May 2007; *Satchmo*, 120-123; and Young homerun in Peter J. Levinson, *Trumpet Blues*, 54. Cole in *Nat King Cole*, 21. Going a step further, cultural historian Gerald Early wrote,

> "I think there are only three things that America will be known for two thousand years from now; the Constitution, jazz music, and baseball, the three most beautifully designed things this country ever produced." Cited in, *Oxford Companion*, 3.

39.) Hamilton background from Junius Rochester, "Doc Hamilton: King of Seattle's Speakeasy Living," in *The Weekly*, 2 February 1983, 37. Hamilton moved to Seattle after serving in World War I with the all-black 92nd Buffalo Division. His first "blind pig" or speakeasy was at 1017 E. Union Street, according to a 1926 *Polk's Directory* listing. Quote and more in Henry Broderick, *First Person Singular*, 49; and in, *A 49 Year Musical History*, 17. Darensbourg description in *Jazz Odyssey*, 68, 72, 76-77, 90. Regarding Darensbourg's use of the word "joint" see "The Jook Joint: An Historical Note," by Graeme Boone and James Clyde Sellman liner notes to Quincy Jones CD *Q's Jook Joint*. Jones comments further about the song *Let The Good Times Roll*,

> "This is a Louis Jordan tune that we used to play as kids in the 40's during World War II in Seattle, Washington in the clubs that would have been the City equivalent to the 'jook joint' (clubs like) the Rockin' Chair, Black & Tan, and the Washington Social Club, which was run by Reverend Silas (sic) Groves." Photo identification from Black Heritage Society Collection MOHAI.

40.) Local 493 early locations, later Blue Note location, & Wells quote in *Calabash*, 86. More addresses found in *IM*, April 1941, 2, Local 493 *Price List* 1949, and *Polk's Seattle Directory* for 1948, 1949, 1951, 1953, 1954, 1955, and 1956. Further detail in Author Interviews with Elmer Gill and Buddy Catlett.

41.) Wells in Tom Stoddard, *Jazz On The Barbary Coast*, ix, 72, 106-109, *Calabash*, 86, and *Jackson Street*, 21. Debate in Regular Meeting of Board of Directors (RMBD) 8 August 1946 and 3 October 1946. A. F. of M. conference in *IM*, April 1941, 2, and in *NWE*, 17 January, and 13 and 27 June 1941. Wells' Jimmie Lunceford show May 21, 1941 at Senator Auditorium in *IM* 16 May 1941. Also see *The Northwest Enterprise* cover story with photo on 5 September 1941 for the 22nd Anniversary "Maestro Wells" show with Erskine Hawkins Big Band. Heartfelt thanks to Ken Steiner for pointing out Wells and 493's Ellington 1940 performance/benefit "Duke & Jim Crow" in *NWE*, 29 March, 1940, 1, 4; and 5 April 1940, 1, 5. Another use of the term occurs in a page one story headlined "War Migration Brings Jim Crow To Northwest" by then freelance writer (and later *Nation* magazine editor) Carey McWilliams in *NWE*, 23 May 1945. Trying to get to the bottom of the first use of the term historian C. Vann Woodward wrote on page 7 of his *The Strange Career of Jim Crow*,

> "The origin of the term 'Jim Crow' applied to Negroes is lost in obscurity. Thomas D. Rice wrote a song and dance called 'Jim Crow' in 1832, and the term had become an adjective by 1838. The first example of 'Jim Crow Law' listed by the *Dictionary of American English* is dated 1904. But the expression was used by writers in the 1890's..."

42.) Payday for 493 from Author Telephone Interview, Carol Maxwell, Local 76-493 Office Secretary, 9 October 1996. Ward quote in Author Interview. Cartoon from *NWE,* 22 March 1944. For a slightly earlier view of black migration to Seattle see Horace Cayton, *Long Old Road,* 1-41, 75-99.

43.) Ogawa photo identification from 1942 and 1943-1944 *Polk's Seattle Directory.* Tip of the hat to Manny Keller-Scholz for long distance research on Ogawa. For further studies in interrelations of Seattle's black and Japanese American communities see *Forging,* 134. Fictional treatment, including mentions of Local 493, in *Hotel on the Corner of Bitter and Sweet* by Jamie Ford.

44.) Seattle World War II era black population growth estimates from *Forging,* 160 and *NWE,* 23 May 1945, 1, 4. Catlett quote in Paul de Barros Interview 9 and 23 November 1988. Further bio details from Author Interview 16 January 1996 including Catlett recalling Joe Darensbourg's music as "the greatest sound I ever heard" at a 1944 Lake Twelve black Merchant Marine event with Ernie Shepweller and Banjoski Adams.

45.) Buddy Groves and Sirless "Sy" Groves data from Author Interview Francis Demisse 22 March 2001. Groves in 493 from Author Interview Viola Howell 22 March 2001. Shantytown gig in *Jackson Street,* 38.

46.) Navy band history from Author Interview William Funderberg and in *Jazz Generations,* by William "Buddy" Collette and Steve Isoardi, 55-60. Jive Bombers from Author Interview John Willis 29 May 1996.

47.) Author Interview William Funderberg. Opposing view from Author Interview Elmer Gill 19 January 1996. Additional details on payment from The Kitty in *Jazz Odyssey,* 72, 74. Special thanks to Burgin Mathews for Funderberg big band photo identification help in email to author 04/10/2024. Further information in Mathews, *Magic City: How the Birmingham Jazz Tradition Shaped the Sound of America,* pp. 122, 124, 192, and 200. Note also that in Birmingham, Funderberg uses the first name of "Howard," but in Seattle he goes by William.

48.) Author Interview William Fundberg. Funderberg, Whatley and Local 733 data from Author Interview Frank "Doc" Adams 22 August 2002, and in M.C. Dickinson "A Teacher of Note: Fess Whatley," 41-44, in *Venues,* August 2002. Whatley protégé and other alums in Whatley, John Fess - Encyclopedia of Alabama https://encyclopediaofalabama.org/article/john-t-fess-whatley/ accessed May 8, 2023.

49.) Union membership and date of birth in Amalgamation List, 14 January 1958. Bob Marshall, is also listed as 493 man in List but not Al Mitchell.. More on Jones in Jane Pugel, "Jazz greats helped pianist find 'Melody'," 3, 24, in *The Progress,* 28 January 1988; *Jackson Street,* 113, 147-149; and Mary Elizabeth Cronin, "Local Jazz Great 'Melody' Jones Is Dead," *Seattle Times,* in http://community.seattletimes.nwsource.com/archive/?date=19960816&slug=2344435. See also "Sweethearts of Jazz," 10. "Kitty" and tips from Author Interview William Funderberg.

50.) Sy Grove history and Lester Young account in Author Interviews Francis Demise and Viola Howell. Seattle Negro Repertory Company from "King County Snapshots," in http://content.lib.washington.edu/cdm-desmo/results.php?CISOOP1=all&CISOBOX1=Sy+Groves. Further detail on Young in Douglas Henry Daniels, *Lester Leaps In: The Life and Times of Lester "Pres" Young,* 267-291. Glassware story in Author Interview Floyd Standifer. See also Author Interviews Ralph Davis 16 and 30 June 2000, and *Jackson Street*, 149. More in Quincy Jones, *Q: The Autobiography of Quincy Jones*, 47-48.

51.) Author Interview Gerald Wiggins 6 February 2008. More in *Jackson Street*, 89-91.

52.) *NWE*, 22 January 1947 for Williams at Washington Social. K.C. riff, L. A. and Portland background, and Pierre quote from *Jumptown*, 82-83. Also in *Jackson Street*, 67, 96. Name bands per Author Interview James T. "Smitty" Smith and Author Interview Kenny Boas, 18 March 2002. Other mentions in *NWE,* 4 April 1945, 27 February and 27 March 1946. Union membership in Amalgamation List.

53.) Author Interview Zenobia Jefferson, 5 June 2001. Author Interview Francis Demise.

54.) "Presumed" since Hickey and Williams were almost certainly members of Local 493. Yet in the only extant listing of 493 union members from 1958, their names do not appear, although they could have been members earlier and dropped out, as others did.

55.) Author Interviews John Willis and Kenny Boas. More on Stewart in Rex Stewart, *Jazz Masters of the Thirties*, 80-103, 209, 223. Ellington in town for Civic Ice Arena show per *NWE,* 26 June 1946.

56.) Bumps in Seattle from *Q* 46-47, and *Jackson Street*, 103-107, 151, 169. Union dispute in RMBD 30 January 1947. Concert in *NWE*, 25 July 1945. Los Angeles material in Roy Porter and David Keller, *There and Back: The Roy Porter Story,* 92-94, 105-106.

57.) Fitzgerald information in Author Interview Ernie Hatfield, 30 March 2000. Early history from Patricia Willard "Ella Fitzgerald, Sarah Vaughan, and Billie Holiday," *Oxford Companion,* 237-239. Webb's death *Encyclopedia of Jazz,* 456. Radio details in Note 22 above.

58.) Concert articles or advertisements in *NWE*, 14 October 1942, 8 September 1943, 27 October 1943, 27 November 1943, 15 December 1943, 3 May 1944, 24 May 1944, 12 July and 21 July 1944, 30 August 1944, 6 September 1944, 15 November 1944, 27 December 1944, 7 February 1945, 24 March 1945, 11 April 1945, 1 and 15 September 1945, 27 February 1946, 3, 10, 16, and 24 April 1946. Seattle show in *NWE* 27 June 1941 and billed as "Fats' Waler's (sic) only Dance Engagement" *NWE* 11 July 1941. Mention of "another coast-to-coast twelve weaker" tour in *Ain't Misbehavin',* 214. Production details in Author Interview Norm Bobrow 18 February 2008 and Paul de Barros Interview with Norm Bobrow 5 July 1989. Waller anecdote in Author Interview Ernie Hatfield.

59.) Extensive treatment in Sherrie Tucker, *Swing Shift*, 63 - 167; D. Antoinette Handy, *The International Sweethearts of Rhythm,* cited in *Swing Shift,* 26; Linda Dahl, *Stormy Weather: The Music and Lives of a Century of Jazzwomen,* 53-57; and in https://nationmaster.com, "Encyclopedia International Sweethearts of Rhythm." More in *Black Beauty,* 308; Geoffrey C. Ward and Ken Burns, *Jazz,* 268; and Gene Fernett, *Swing Out,* 166. Eddie Durham and All Star Girl Orchestra in Seattle from *NWE,* 24 May 1944. Photo identification help provided by Sherrie Tucker in email to author 16 August 2008. See also "Sweethearts of Jazz," 9.

60.) Jones background in *Jackson Street,* 62, 69-70. Newspaper account in *NWE,* 14 October 1942. Clip from *NWE* 30 June 1943.

61-64.) Performances in *NWE,* 14 October 1942, 8 September, 27 October, 17 November 1943, 3 and 24 May, 12 and 21 July, 27 December 1944, 7 February 1945, 3 April, 4 and 25 September 1946. Additional Armstrong and Calloway concert specifics from J. Willis Sayre Photograph Collection in University of Washington Libraries, Special Collections. Further notes on Cab Calloway's bus travel perils in the South during World War II era in *Swing Shift,* 138. See Note 28 re: "Featherbedding," and Note 40 above re: 493 location in Wells home. Ads in *NWE,* 8 September 1943.

65.) Hackett notes in *Jackson Street*, 62, 69-70. See Note 35 above re: union membership.

66) White, jitterbug, and Palomar items from www.streetswing.com, and Sonny Watson's Streetswing.com, "The Jitterbug," 1. See also www.Centralhome.com, Lori Heikkila, "History of Swing Dancing," 1-3. Ban on jitterbugging from Chuck Cecil radio program, "The Swingin' Years," broadcast on KKJZ FM 5 July 2008 7:30 A.M. Dick Clark incident from www.people.cornell.edu, Kurt Lichtmann, "50's Jitterbug," 1. Tolles quote from "Jazz on the Spot."

67.) Boas fine in Regular Meeting Executive Board (RMEB) 7 November 1944, and detail in Boas Author Interview. Blackwell and turf in Regular Meeting of Board of Directors (RMBD) 28 June 1945. Black and Tan on list and Wells' response in RMEB 23 June 1945. Colored Waiters, Porters, and Cooks Club in *NWE,* 7 August 1946, 1.

68.) Bulosan description from *America Is,* 104-105. Fuller and band in "Jazz on The Spot," and *Jackson Street,* 142. Union membership identification from "New Members List." Boyd in Author Interview, Gerald Wiggins.

69-70.) Bobrow and Wells in Author Interviews, and in de Barros Norm Bobrow Interview. Swing concert in *Seattle Star,* 5 February 1940 and *Seattle Times* 2 December 1940. Bobrow fine and Wells club debated in RMBD 8 August and 3 October 1946. Rinaldi in Special Minutes Executive Board 30 March 1937. See also Note 23 when Rinaldi played in a mixed race band in 1932, possibly joining 493 then. Rinaldi was a first-call sideman for years, also gigging with Joe Darensbourg at a tough saloon called the Silver Dollar in unionized Grand Coulee, Washington during the construction of the Grand Coulee Dam. Darensbourg's band worked there from 9:00 PM until 1:00 AM and then went across the street to "play at an after-hours joint owned by a colored guy named Moses Johnson," in *Jazz Odyssey,* 92-93, and *Jackson Street,* 38. Later in 1938, Rinaldi lived in Grand Coulee and was a director at its Local 397, see *IM,* March 1938, Volume 36, 18. More on the Silver Dollar and Grand Coulee in *Before Seattle Rocked,* 122-123. See also Note 24. Ernestine Anderson Equity affiliation from 19 October 2008 and 10 April 2009 Jacqueline E.A. Lawson emails to author. See also "Sweethearts of Jazz," 11.

71-75.) Club background from Author Interview Elmer Gill. Quote from de Barros Elmer Gill Author Interview. Contrast Gill's fondness for clubs with the detailed attack, though marred by political jargon, in Frank Kofsky's, *Black Nationalism and the Revolution in Music*, particularly chapter six, "The Jazz Club," 145-154.

76.) Turay quote from Author Interview, Al Hilbert background and Hilbert quotes from Author Interview Dorothy Hilbert. More on Hilbert in *Jackson Street,* 77-78, 80.

77.) Quincy with Hamp in *Q,* 65-66, 72-74. Thurlow and Gill from *Jackson Street,* 83-86, 142-145, and

Gill Author Interview. Rope cutting in *Hamp*, 98. Richardson quote in *Q*, 73. Jacquet photo identification from Lionel Hampton at Seattle Civic Auditorium 1946 - Bing images MOHAI, accessed 04/28/2023.

78-80.) Importance of economic boom in Harvard Sitkoff, *A New Deal for Blacks*, 211-230. Whites and others could join Local 493, but except for Powell Barnett no other black musician ever joined Local 76. White members included Bill Rinaldi, Traff Hubert, Mike DeFillipis, Fred Greenwell, Kenny Boas, and Jan Skugstad. See above Notes 23, 68 and 70-71. Boas, DeFillipis and Skugstad in Amalgamation list January 14, 1958. More from Author Interviews Buddy Catlett, John Willis, Jabo Ward, Floyd Standifer, and Kenny Boas. See also *Jackson Street,* 60-67. Hawaiian-surnamed members Edmond Kamai and Olino Kaulili listed as new members of 493 in the *IM*, March 1943, 20. Hispanic surnamed, Elsie Martínez is listed in the 1958 Local 493 Amalgamation List. Hatfield quotes and background from Author Interview.

81-82.) Union locations in Note 40 above. Plywood description, drink prices, and quote from Author Interview Buddy Catlett. Cruise and Brown friendships in *Jackson Street,* 62-65. Standifer quote in Author Interview. Officials and supporters as listed on Ernie Hatfield image.

83.) Ernie Hatfield information from musicians' union membership cards.

84-85.) Born on 23 September 1930, Charles arrival in Seattle "around March of 1948" makes him 17. Seattle trip detailed in Ray Charles and David Ritz *Brother Ray*, 92-95. Jones account from *Jackson Street*, 149-150. Early work as Maxim Trio from Clive Richardson liner notes to the album "20 Golden Pieces of Ray Charles," Bulldog Records, BDL 2012, where Charles is heard in Nat Cole style. More in *Jackson Street*, 150-152, and *Brother Ray*, 97 where the trio is alternately named the Maxin or McSon Trio. Dorothy Hilbert quote from Author Interview. Charles labels The Rocking Chair as his first gig as part of a talent contest from which he found steady work at the black Elks Club, in *Brother Ray*, 97, and plays a slow, soulful composition in honor of the club. "Rockin' Chair Blues" on "20 Golden Pieces." Zenobia Jefferson confirmed the "humble beginnings" of Charles, see page 100 above, Author Interview. Press mention in *NWE*, 15 June 1949. The Marjorie Polk Sotero photographs were discovered in a search at the Douglas-Truth Branch of the Seattle Public Library. (Photographer Marjorie Polk Sotero began work at Camp Jordan as the Director of the 6th Army Service Club in 1944 per Jacqueline E. A. Lawson, *Camp George Jordan*, 15.) "Service Club No. 2" had previously been known as "Colored 85-Service Club," *Camp George Jordan*, 14. Both photographs are credited to Sgt. William L. Logan as U.S. Army Photograph, 9779-123-1/AM 50 and 9779-123-3/AM 50 14 respectively.

86.) Sotero background in *Camp George Jordan*. Photograph is P000-028 with no photographer listed. Buffalo Soldiers information from *African American Cultural Guide*, "Fort Lawton Historic District, Discovery Park," 2008, not paginated. Fort Lawton background from *Forging*, 143, 147. More detail in Heather MacIntosh, Priscilla Long, and David Wilma "Riot involving African American soldiers occurs at Fort Lawton and an Italian POW is lynched on August 14, 1944," http://www.historylink.org/. See also Jack Hamann, *On American Soil: How Justice Became A Casualty of World War II*, and "Three Deny Guilt at Ft. Lawton Trial," *Seattle Times*, 18 August 1944, 2, and from "Riot Involving." Update from Kim Murphy, "Justice, 64 Years Later," *Los Angeles Times*, 27 July 2008, A16, and Angie Leventis Lourgos, "Convicted WWII veteran gets justice before dying," *Los Angeles Times*, 16 December 2012, A28.

87.) Ft. Lawton background, and quote from *Jackson Street*, 112-113, and unpaginated photo section. See also "Remembering: Patti Bown A Woman, A Piano, A Storm," http://www.schillingersociety.com/index.php?option=com_content&view=article&id=61&Itemid=73, and Doug Ramsey, "Patti Bown,"

Rifftides, 25 March 2008, http://www.artsjournal.com/rifftides/2008/03/patti_bown.html.

88-89.) Tuxedo Club infraction in RMBD 21 March 1950. Drift Inn and other infractions in RMBD 4 June, 8 October 1953, 19 April 1956. Thunderbird dispute in RMBD 14 June 1956. Los Angeles merger from Marl Young "The Amalgamation of Locals 47 and 767," *Overture,* 8, 9. More in William Douglass *Central Avenue Sounds,* 182-190. Contrasting experience of Chicago in Clark Halker, "A History of Local 208 and the Struggle for Racial Equality," *Black Music Research Journal* 1988, 207-221. Comparisons of Los Angeles Local 767 and Chicago's 208 in David Keller, *Seattle's Segregated Musicians' Union, Local 493, 1918-1956,* 128-164. See also "Racial Segregation and the San Francisco Musicians' Union," 161-206. Seattle 493 and 76 meetings in RMBD 18 August 1949 and 14 September 1949. See also Monthly Meeting of Musicians' Association (MMMA) 10 October 1949, 9 November 1949, and 11 January 1950. On 8 February 1950 MMMA amalgamation matter "tabled indefinitely." Amalgamation action continued on 8 July 1954 RMBD when liaison committee from 76 charged to meet with 493 committee on amalgamation. More merger meetings in MMMA 10 August 1954.

89-90.) when Powell Barnett notes formation of 493 committee. More in RMBD 19 August 1954 with progress noted by 76 President Reed. 12 October and 9 November 1954 meetings in MMMA. At latter, amalgamation arrangements and Local 493 favorable vote noted. No activity until MMMA 13 March 1956 when 76 President Martin announces new amalgamation committee. RMED 8 November 1956 request to notify "The Federation" about the proposed amalgamation of two locals. Specific proposal and committee members noted at same meeting. See also "Amalgamation of the Colored," 5, 6. More in Powell Barnett Manuscripts, "Volunteers of America," 2, and "Amalgamation of the Colored," 22-23, re: Gerald Wells contacting Barnett, and Wells' "dictatorial style." Thunderbird Club dispute in RMBD 14 June 1956. Breakfast Jam in Gill and Turay Author Interviews. L. A. comparison from Tadd Hershorn Telephone interview, Norman Granz, 11 March 2000 and Patricia Willard interview, Norman Granz, 23 August 1989.

90-92.) See above Note 87 for 1954 actions. Amalgamation vote scheduled for December 15, 1956, in General Meeting Minutes 13 November 1956. Editorial pleas and list in *Musicland* December 1956, 1. Favorable Local 76 vote reported in "Amalgamation of the Colored," 6. More in 76 work file, 14 January 1958, Local 76-493. Gill and Funderberg intra-union anti-merger votes in Author Interviews, Hatfield quote in Author Interview. Details confirmed in *Seattle Times,* 19 January 1959, 33.

93.) Background and quote in Author Interview Floyd Standifer. For "Rainbow Coalition" members at Blue Note see Notes 23, 68, 70-71, and 79-81, above. DeFillipis in Amalgamation list January 14, 1958. More from Author Interviews Buddy Catlett, John Willis, Jabo Ward, Floyd Standifer, and Kenny Boas. See also *Jackson Street,* 60 – 67.

94-96.) Pete's and Ward from Author Interview Jabo Ward. See also *Jackson Street,* 195-196, 198-199. Thanks to Doug Barnett for Penthouse suggestion. Coltrane at the Penthouse from Keith Raether, "Out of this World, John Coltrane in Seattle," *Earshot Jazz,* April 1995, in www.hipcity.com. More in Bill Cole, *John Coltrane,* 177, and J. C. Thomas, *Chasin' the Trane: The Music and Mystique of John Coltrane,* 251.

98-100.) The Door, Colony, Q. Jones, Bostic, and Aqua Jazz history from Author Interviews Ben Laigo, 10 May 2000 and 1 March 2001. Bostic's fame at this time in *Who's Who of Jazz,* 42.

100-101.) Don Osias strange times in Montana from Author Interview Don Osias. More thanks to Milt Krieger for Ken Robison's "Breaking Racial Barriers 'Everyone's Welcome' At The Ozark Club," *Montana: The Magazine of Western History,* Summer 2012, 44-58. Thanks as well to Ken Robison for research in the *Great Falls Tribune* and its Saturday ads from 12 September through December 19, 1959 confirming Roberts Quartet "fresh from Nino's 440 Club in San Francisco" at the Ozark. Roberts' music and background from Andy Grigg, "Frank Roberts: Seattle's Tenor Sax Legend," in *Real Blues* Parts I and II, June/July 1999, Number 19, 38-39, 76, and August/September, 1999, Number 20, 29-31. Roberts mentions that all of the "talented" neighborhood kids, who'd grown up watching Buddy Catlett, Quincy Jones, and Ray Charles among others "were put into the musicians' union (493) for free," *Real Blues,* 76. Dallas Schachere in 493 from "New Members List," 1958.

102.) Author Interviews, Buddy Catlett and Floyd Standifer; and *Q,* 135-145. "Dead broke" from "Living It" by Buddy Catlett in *Q,* 147. Special thanks to Douglas Q. Barnett and Jacqueline E.A. Lawson who caught the published misidentification of trumpeter Floyd Standifer with Lennie Johnson in the "Free and Easy" photograph.

103.) Hilbert background in Author Interview Dorothy Hilbert. See also Notes 10-11. Legal alcohol in *Session Laws of the State of Washington 1949,* Chapter Five. Howell quote from Author Interview Viola Howell.

104.) Barnett union membership in Note 5. See Notes 8 and 9 also for Local 458 information. More in Author Interview Douglass Q. Barnett. For a summary of Barnett's other contributions to the civic life of Seattle, see also "Powell Barnett" in Mary T. Henry and Marilyn H. Henry's *Tribute : A Guide to Seattle's Public Parks and Buildings Named for Black People,* 57-59.

Bibliography

INTERVIEWS

Author Interview. Frank "Doc" Adams. 22 August 2002. Birmingham, AL.

Author Interviews. Douglas Q. Barnett. 3 March 2000, and 2 March 2001. Seattle, WA.

Author Interview. Kenny Boas. 18 March 2002. Seattle, WA.

Author Telephone Interview. Norm Bobrow. 18 February 2008. Seattle, WA.

Norm Bobrow Interview by Paul de Barros. 5 July 1989. Seattle, WA.

Author Interview. George James "Buddy" Catlett. 16 January 1996. Seattle, WA.

George James "Buddy" Catlett Interview by Paul de Barros. 9 and 23 November 1988. Seattle, WA.

Author Interviews. Ralph Davis. 16 and 30 June 2000. Seattle, WA.

Author Interview. Francis Demisse. 22 March, 19 April 2001. Seattle, WA.

Bill Douglass Interview by Steve Isoardi, part of *Central Avenue Sounds* project, U.C.L.A. Oral History Program, 1993. Los Angeles, CA.

Author Interview. William Funderberg. 20 May 1996. Seattle, WA.

Author Interview. Elmer Gill. 19 January 1996. Bellingham, WA.

Elmer Gill Interview by Paul de Barros. 28 October 1988. Gibson's Landing, B.C.

Author Interview. Roy Green. 5 March 1996. Bellingham, WA.

Norman Granz Interview, by Tad Hershorn. 11 March 2000. Author Telephone Interview with Hershorn.

Norman Granz Interview, by Patricia Willard. 23 August 1989. Duke Ellington Collection, Smithsonian Institution, Washington D.C.

Author Interviews. Ernie Hatfield. 30 March and 16 June 2000. Seattle, WA.

Author Interview. Dorothy Hilbert. 18 February 2000. Seattle, WA.

Author Interview. Viola Howell. 22 March, 19 April 2001. Seattle, WA

Author Telephone Interview. Zenobia Jefferson. 5 June 2001.

Author Interview. Beverly Kelly. 24 February 2000. Seattle, WA.

Author Interviews. Ben Laigo. 10 May 2000 and 1 March 2001. Seattle, WA.

Author Telephone Interview. Jacqueline E.A. Lawson. 22 April, 12 June 2008.

Charles Lewis Interview by Esther Mumford. Oral/Aural History Collection, Washington State Archives. 20 August 1975. Olympia, WA.

Author Interviews. Dorothy Lomax. 22 March, 19 April 2001. Seattle, WA.

Author Interview. Dan Mather. 20 November 2000. Bellingham, WA.

Author Telephone Interview. Carol Maxwell. 9 October 1996.

Author Interview. Don Osias. 30 March 2000. Seattle WA.

Author Interview. Frank Osias. 30 March 2000. Seattle WA.

Author Interview. Al Smith. 30 June 2000. Seattle, WA.

Author Interview. James T. "Smitty" Smith. 10 March 2000. Seattle, WA.

Author Interview. Karen Smith Surall. 20 April 2001. Seattle, WA.

Author Interview. Floyd Standifer. 16 January 1996. Seattle, WA.

Author Interview. Al Turay. 20 April 2001. Des Moines, WA.

Author Interview. Ulysses G. "Jabo" Ward. 20 May 1996. Seattle, WA.

Author Interview. Gerald "Wig" Wiggins. 6 February 2008. Woodland Hills, CA.

Author Interview. John Willis. 29 May 1996. Seattle, WA.

AUTOBIOGRAPHIES

Armstrong, Louis, *Louis Armstrong, in His Own Words: Selected Writings*. Edited by Thomas Brothers. New York: Oxford University Press, 1999.

Broderick, Henry. *First Person Singular*. Seattle: F. McCaffrey and His Dogwood Press, 1943.

Cayton, Horace. *Long Old Road: An Autobiography*. Seattle: University of Washington Press, 1963. Washington Paperback edition, 1970.

Charles, Ray and Ritz, David. *Brother Ray: Ray Charles, Own Story*. New York: The Dial Press, 1978.

Collette, William "Buddy" and Steve Isoardi, *Jazz Generations: A Life In American Music and Society*. London: Continuum International Publishing Group, 2000.

Darensbourg, Joe, with Vacher, Peter. *A Jazz Odyssey: The Autobiography of Joe Darensbourg*. Baton Rouge: Louisiana State University Press, 1987.

Hampton, Lionel with Haskins, James. *Hamp: An Autobiography*. New York: Warner Books, 1989.

Jones, Quincy. *Q: The Autobiography of Quincy Jones*. New York: Doubleday, 2001.

Porter, Roy with David Keller. *There and Back: The Roy Porter Story*. Baton Rouge: Louisiana State University Press, 1991.

MANUSCRIPT & PHOTOGRAPH COLLECTIONS

Mary E. Adams Collection, Accession No. 1165, Special Collections, Manuscripts & University Archives Division, University of Washington Libraries, Seattle, WA.

American Federation of Musicians Local 76 Records including: *Amalgamation List, Board Meeting Minutes, Monthly Meeting Minutes, Regular Meeting of Executive Board, Regular Meeting of the Associated Minutes, Regular Meeting of the Board of Directors, Special Board Meeting Minutes, Special Meeting of Executive Board,* 1913-1958, Union Headquarters, A. F. of M. Local 76-493, Seattle, WA.

Black Heritage Society of Washington State, Inc. Collection, Museum of History & Industry Seattle, WA.

Marjorie Polk Sotero Photographs, Seattle Public Library, Douglass-Truth Branch, Seattle, WA

J. Willis Sayre Photograph Collection in University of Washington Libraries, Special Collections, Seattle, WA

Roslyn Black History, Local History Collection, Ellensburg Public Library, Ellensburg, WA.

Powell Barnett Manuscripts, Accession No. 721, Special Collections, Manuscripts & University Archives Division, University of Washington Libraries, Seattle, WA.

PUBLICATIONS

African American Cultural Guide. First Edition 2008. Seattle, WA.

American Music. Winter, 1985. Urbana, IL.

BlackPast.org., 18 July 2010. Seattle, WA

The Cascade Miner. 24 October 1908. Roslyn, WA.

Cayton's Monthly. February 1920. Seattle, WA.

Columbia Magazine. Winter 2009-10, Tacoma, WA.

Earshot Jazz. April 1995. Seattle, WA.

Great Falls Tribune. September-December, 1959. Great Falls, MT.

International Musician. 1912-1965. St. Louis, MO and New York, NY.

Jackson Street Community Council Newsletter. 15 October 1963. Seattle, WA.

Journal of the Society for American Music. May 2007. Cambridge, England.

Los Angeles Times. 27 July 2008, 16 December 2012. Los Angeles, CA.

Montana The Magazine of Western History. Summer 2012. Helena, MT.

Musicland. 1921-1931. Seattle, WA.

The Northwest Enterprise. 1921-1954. Seattle, WA.

Overture. December 1988, Los Angeles, CA.

The Progress. 28 January 1988, Seattle, WA.

Real Blues. June-September 1999. Victoria, B.C., Canada.

The Seattle Medium. 14 February 1974. Seattle, WA.

Seattle Post-Intelligencer. 2 May 1964. Seattle, WA.

Seattle Star. 5 January 1940. Seattle, WA.

Seattle Times. 1917, 1940-1949, 1959, 1996. Seattle, WA.

Session Laws of the State of Washington 1949. Olympia, WA.

Spawn of Coal Dust: History of Roslyn, 1886-1955. Operation Uplift, Community Development Program, 1955. Roslyn, WA.

Through Open Eyes. Ellensburg Public Library. Ellensburg, WA.

Venues. August 2002. Birmingham, AL.

The Weekly. 2 February 1983. Seattle, WA.

OTHER WORKS CITED

Albertson, Chris. *Bessie.* New York: Stein and Day Publishers, 1972.

———. "Bessie Smith," in *The Oxford Companion to Jazz.* Edited by Bill Kirchner. New York: Oxford University Press, 2000.

All About Shanghai and Environs A Standard Guide Book. 1934-1935. Reprint. Taipei: Che'Eng Wen Publishing Company, 1973.

Armbruster, Kurt E. *Before Seattle Rocked: A City and Its Music.* Seattle: University of Washington Press, 2011.

Berger, Kenny. "Coleman Hawkins," in *The Oxford Companion to Jazz.* Edited by Bill Kirchner. New York: Oxford University Press, 2000.

Berner, Richard C. *Seattle 1921-1940: From Boom to Bust.* Seattle: Charles Press, 1992.

Blecha, Peter. "Birdland: Seattle's Fabled 1950s R&B Hotspot," HistoryLink.org Online Encyclopedia of Washington State History, http://www.historylink.org/.

———. "'Jazz Intoxication' bill is introduced in Washington State Legislature on December 22, 1933," HistoryLink.org Online Encyclopedia of Washington State History, http://www.historylink.org/.

Boone, Graeme, and Sellman, James Clyde, "The Jook Joint: An Historical Note," liner notes to Quincy Jones compact disc *Q's Jook Joint*. Quest/UMG, 1994.

Brothers, Thomas, Editor. *Louis Armstrong, In His Own Words: Selected Writings*. New York: Oxford University Press, 1999.

Brown, Charles E. "Al Smith Jr., Photographer, Historian." *Seattle Times*. 5 September 2008.

Bulosan, Carlos. *America Is In The Heart*. Seattle: University of Washington Press, 1996.

Campbell, Mary Schmidt; Driskell, David; Lewis; David Levering, Ryan; Willis, Deborah, editors. *Harlem Renaissance: Art of Black America*. New York: Abradale Press, 1994.

Carr, Ian, Digby Fairweather, Brian Priestley, Chris Parker, John Corbett, Jeff Kaliss, Richard Plant, et al. Jazz : The Rough Guide. London: Rough Guides, 1995.

Cave, Mark. "Jelly Roll Morton: Shoe Shiner's Drag," *Jazz Scrapbook: Bill Russell and Some Highly Musical Friends*. New Orleans: Historic New Orleans Collection, 1998.

Cecil, Chuck. "The Swingin' Years," Radio broadcast on KKJZ FM Radio, 5 July 2008, 7:30 AM.

Chilton, John. *Who's Who of Jazz: Storyville to Swing Street*. Time-Life Records Special Edition, 1978.

Cole, Bill. *John Coltrane*. New York: Schirmer Books, 1976.

Collier, James Lincoln. *Duke Ellington*. New York: Oxford University Press, 1987.

Cordova, Fred. *Filipinos, Forgotten Asian Americans: A Pictorial Essay 1763-circa 1963*. Seattle: Demonstration Project for Asian Americans, 1983.

Dahl, Linda. *Morning Glory: A Biography of Mary Lou Williams*. Berkeley: University of California Press, 2001.

———. *Stormy Weather: The Music and Lives of a Century of Jazzwomen*. Reprint. London: Quartet Books, 1990.

Dance, Stanley. *The World of Earl Hines*. New York: Scribner, 1977.

Daniels, Douglas Henry. *Lester Leaps In: The Life and Times of Lester "Pres" Young*. Boston: Beacon Press, 2002.

De Barros, Paul. *Jackson Street After Hours: The Roots of Jazz in Seattle*. Seattle: Sasquatch Books, 1993.

De Barros, Paul and Giske, Howard. "Jazz On The Spot: The Photography of Al Smith," Museum of History and Industry exhibit, Seattle: September 1993.

De Barros, Paul. "One Symphony Musician Grew Up Playing With Harlem's Greats," *Seattle Times*. 30 May 2002.

Del Fiornetino, Dan. *Big Bands Database Plus*. http://www.info.net/usa/c5.html.

DeVeaux, Scott. *The Birth of Bebop: A Social and Musical History*. Berkeley and Los Angeles: University of California Press, 1997.

Dickinson, M.C. "A Teacher of Note: Fess Whatley," *Venues,* August, 41-44, 2002

Dietsche, Robert. *Jumptown The Golden Years of Portland Jazz, 1942-1957*. Corvallis: Oregon State University Press, 2005.

http://www.digitalarchives.wa.gov Database: Spokane County Marriage Records.

Driggs, Frank and Lewine, Harris. *Black Beauty, White Heat: A Pictorial History of Classic Jazz 1920-1950*. New York: William Morrow and Company, 1982.

Duncan, Don. "Last Attraction: Death of the Orpheum," *Seattle Times,* n.d.

Early, Gerald. Introduction in *The Oxford Companion to Jazz*. Edited by Bill Kirchner. New York: Oxford University Press, 2000.

Encyclopedia of Alabama, Whatley, John Fess-Encyclopedia of Alabama, https://encyclopediaofalabama.org/article/john-t-fess-whatley/.

Feather, Leonard. *The Encyclopedia of Jazz*. New York: Bonanza Books, 1960.

Fernett, Gene. *Swing Out: Great Negro Dance Bands*. 1970. Reprint. New York: Da Capo Press, 1993.

Ford, Jamie. *Hotel on the Corner of Bitter and Sweet*. 2009. New York: Ballantine Books.

Gabbard, Krin. *Jammin' at the Margins: Jazz and the American Cinema*. Chicago: The University of Chicago Press, 1996.

Gerard, Charley. *Jazz in Black & White Race: Culture, and Identity in the Jazz Community*. Westport, CT: Praeger Publishers, 1998.

Giddins, Gary. *Bing Crosby: A Pocketful of Dreams: The Early Years 1903-1940*. Boston: Little, Brown and Company, 2001.

———. *Satchmo*. Reprint. New York: Da Capo Press, 1998.

Gioia, Ted. *The History of Jazz*. New York: Oxford University Press, 1997.

Grigg, Andy. "Frank Roberts: Seattle's Tenor Sax Legend," *Real Blues,* 19, 20: 29-31, 38-39, 76. 1999.

Gushee, Lawrence. "A Preliminary Chronology of the Early Career of Ferd 'Jelly Roll' Morton," *American Music* 3: 405-408. 1985.

Hackenmiller, Tom. *Labor Unions in the Upper Kittitas County, 1884-1894,* Unpublished Master's Thesis, Central Washington Branch Washington State Archives. 1989.

Halker, Clark. "A History of Local 208 and the Struggle for Racial Equality," *Black Music Research Journal,* 8: 89-90. 1988.

Hamann, Jack. *On American Soil: How Justice Became A Casualty of World War II*. Reprint. Seattle: University of Washington Press, 2007

Harris, William H., and Levey, Judith S. *The New Columbia Encyclopedia*. New York: Columbia University Press, 1975.

Harrison, Daphne Duval. *Black Pearls: Blues Queens of the 1920s*. New Brunswick, NJ: Rutgers University Press, 1990.

Haskins, Jim. *The Cotton Club*. Reprint. New York: Hippocrene Books, Paperback edition, 1994.

Haskins, Jim with Kathleen Benson. *Nat King Cole*. Briarcliff Manor, NY: Stein and Day Publishers: 1984.

Henry, Mary T., and Marilyn H. Henry. *Tribute : A Guide to Seattle's Public Parks and Buildings Named for Black People: With Brief Biographical Sketches*. Seattle: Statice Press, 1997.

Hentoff, Nat. *Jazz Is*. New York: Avon Books: 1976.

Heikkala, Lori. "History of Swing Dancing," 1-3. www.Centralhome.com.

Jewell, Derek. *Duke: A Portrait of Duke Ellington*. New York: W. W. Norton & Company, 1977.

Keepnews, Orrin, Grauer, Bill, Jr. *A Pictorial History of Jazz: People and Places from New Orleans to the Sixties*. Reprint. New York: Bonanza Books, 1981.

Keller, David. "Sweethearts of Jazz: The Women of Seattle's Black Musicians' Unions," *Columbia,* Volume 23, No. 4, 6-12, Winter 2009-10.

———. "Race, Gender, Jazz & Local 493: Black Women Musicians in Seattle, 1920-1955," *BlackPast.org,*

18 July 2010.

———. *Seattle's Segregated Musicians' Union, Local 493, 1918-1956.* Unpublished Master's Thesis, Northwest Regional Branch, Washington State Archives, 1996.

Kenney, William Howland. *Chicago Jazz: A Cultural History, 1904-1930.* New York: Oxford University Press, 1993.

———. *Recorded Music In American Life: The Phonograph and Popular Memory, 1890-1945.* New York: Oxford University Press, 1999.

Kirkeby, Ed. *Ain't Misbehavin': The Story of Fats Waller.* Reprint. New York: Da Capo Press, 1985.

Kofsky, Frank. *Black Nationalism and the Revolution in Music.* New York: Pathfinder Press, 1970.

Lawson, Jacqueline, E. A. *Let's Take a Walk! A Tour of Seattle's Central Area, As It Was Then: 1920s and 1930s.* Seattle: 1997.

———. *A Story of Camp George Jordan: A Black U.S. Army Camp During World War II in Seattle, Washington.* Seattle: 2007.

Levinson. Peter J. *Trumpet Blues: The Life of Harry James.* New York: Oxford University Press, 1999.

Lichtmann, Kurt. "50's Jitterbug," 1, www.people.cornell.edu.

Lomax, Alan. *Mister Jelly Roll: The Fortunes of Jelly Roll Morton, New Orleans Creole and "Inventor of Jazz."* Reprint. Berkeley: University of California Press, 2001.

Lourgos, Angie Leventis, "Convicted WWII Veteran Gets Justice Before Dying," *Los Angeles Times.* 16 December 2012, A28.

Lovell, Charles. *Through Open Eyes: Ninety-Five Years of Black History in Roslyn, Washington.* Ellensburg Public Library, n.d.

MacDonald, Wally. *A 49 Year Musical History of the Northwest.* Seattle: 1995.

MacIntosh, Heather; Long, Priscilla; Wilma, David. "Riot Involving African American Soldiers Occurs at Fort Lawton and an Italian POW is Lynched on August 14, 1944," HistoryLink.org, http://www.historylink.org/.

McWilliams, Carey. Introduction to *America Is In The Heart* by Carlos Bulosan. Seattle: University of Washington Press, 1996.

Mathews, Burgin. *Magic City: How the Birmingham Jazz Tradition Shaped the Sound of America.* Chapel Hill: The University of North Carolina Press, 2023.

Mattfeld, Julius. *Variety Music Cavalcade Musical-Historical Review 1620-1969: A Chronology of Vocal and Instrumental Music Popular in the United States.* Englewood Cliffs, N.: Prentice-Hall, Inc., 1971.

Meeker, David. *Jazz in the Movies.* London: Talisman Books, 1981.

Miller, Leta E. "Racial Segregation and the San Francisco Musicians' Union, 1923-60," *Journal of the Society for American Music,* 2007. 161-206

Miller, Mark. *Jazz In Canada: Fourteen Lives.* Reprint. Toronto: Nightwood Editions, 1988.

Moyses, Sean. "Eddie Peabody 1902-1970," http://www.redhotjazz.com//peabody.html.

Mumford, Esther Hall. *Calabash: A Guide to the History, Culture and Art of African Americans in Seattle and King County Washington.* Seattle: Ananse Press, 1993.

Murphy, Kim. "Justice, 64 Years Later." *Los Angeles Times.* July 27, 2008: A16.

National Archives. 1910 Federal Population Census, http://www.archives.gov/research/census/publications-microfilm-catalogs-census/1910/index.html 2007.

http://nationmaster.com, "Encyclopedia – International Sweethearts of Rhythm."

Oliphant, Dave. "Eugene Coy," *Handbook of Texas Online*, http://www.tsha.utexas.edu/handbook/online/articles/CC/fcods.html.

Pastras, Phil. *Dead Man Blues: Jelly Roll Morton Way Out West*. Berkeley and Chicago: University of California Press and Center For Black Music Research, 2001.

Peabody, Eddie. "Painting the Clouds With Sunshine," and "The Hal Kemp Band with Eddie Peabody," www.youtube.com.

Pitts, Robert Bradford. *Organized Labor and the Negro in Seattle*, Unpublished Master's Thesis. University of Washington, 1941.

Polk's Seattle Directory. Seattle: R.L. Polk, & Co. 1918 –1944.

Polk's Seattle, King County, Washington. Seattle: R.L. Polk, & Co. 1948-1956.

Polk's Spokane Directory. Spokane: R.L. Polk, & Co. 1895-1920.

Poston, Ken. *Swing Into Spring*. Los Angeles Jazz Institute: May 2007.

Price List and Working Rules. Seattle: Musicians' Protective Union of Seattle Local 493, 1949.

Priestly, Brian. *Jazz On Record: A History*. New York: Billboard Books, 1991.

Raether, Keith. "Out of this World; John Coltrane in Seattle," *Earshot Jazz*, April 1995, www.hipcity.com.

Ramsey, Doug, "Patti Bown," *Rifftides*, 25 March 2008, www.artsjournal.com/rifftides/2008/03/patti_bown.html.

Reed, Ishmael. *The Reed Reader*. New York: Basic Books, 2000.

Richardson, Clive. Notes from "20 Golden Pieces of Ray Charles," Bulldog Records, BDL 2012.

Robertson, Brian. *Little Blues Book*. Chapel Hill, NC: Algonquin Books, 1996.

Robison, Ken. "Breaking Racial Barriers 'Everyone's Welcome' At The Ozark Club." *Montana: The Magazine of Western History*. 62, No. 2:44-58. Summer 2012.

Rochester, Junius. "Doc Hamilton: King of Seattle's Speakeasy Living." *The Weekly*, 8:37-38. 2 February 1983.

Russell, Ross. *Jazz Style in Kansas City and the Southwest*. Berkeley: University of California Press, 1971.

Schillinger Society. "Remembering: Patti Bown A woman, A piano, and a Storm," http://www.schillingersociety.com/index.php?option=com_content&view=article&id=61&Itemid=73.

Schuller, Gunther. *Early Jazz: Its Roots and Musical Development*. Reprint. New York: Oxford University Press, 1986.

———. *The Swing Era The Development of Jazz, 1930-1945*. Reprint. New York: Oxford University Press, 1991.

Sergeant, Harriet. *Shanghai Collision: Point of Cultures, 1918-1939*. New York: Crown Publishers, 1990.

Siegl, Eleanor. *The Amalgamation of the Colored and White Musicians' Unions in Seattle*. Unpublished University of Washington Sociology 462 paper and correspondence. Local 76-493 Union Headquarters, 1966.

Sitkoff, Harvard. *A New Deal for Blacks: The Emergence of Civil Rights as a National Issue, Volume 1 The Depression Decade*. New York: Oxford University Press, 1978.

Smith, Parson Catherine. "William Grant Still Dean of Afro-American Composers," in *Music In The Central Avenue Community 1890-c.1955*. Edited by Bette Y. Cox.. Los Angeles: The Beem Foundation for the Advancement of Music. 1996.

Smith, Merle Irene. *Seattle Had A Tin Pan Alley, Too!* Seattle: Merle I. Smith, 1989.

Southern, Eileen. *The Music of Black Americans: A History*. New York: W. W. Norton, 1971.

Starr, Frederick S. *Red and Hot: The Fate of Jazz in the Soviet Union*. Reprint. New York: Limelight Editions, 1985.

Stewart, Rex. *Jazz Masters of the Thirties*. Reprint. New York: Da Capo Press, 1980.

Stoddard, Tom. *Jazz On The Barbary Coast*. Reprint. Berkeley: Heyday Books, 1998.

Sudhalter, Richard. Liner notes to "The Jazz Age New York in the Twenties," RCA Bluebird CD, 1991.

———. *Lost Chords: White Musicians and Their Contribution to Jazz, 1915-1945*. New York: Oxford University Press, 1998.

Taylor, Quintard. *The Forging of a Black Community: Seattle's Central District from 1870 through the Civil Rights Era*. Seattle: University of Washington Press, 1993.

———. *In Search of the Racial Frontier: African Americans in the American West, 1528-1990*. New York: W. W. Norton, 1998.

Thomas, J.C. *Chasin' the Trane: The Music and Mystique of John Coltrane*. Reprint. New York: Da Capo Press, 1977.

Tomkins, Les. "Jazz Professional Ben Webster Talking to Les Tomkins in 1965." www.jazzprofessional.com/interviews/BenWebster.htm.

Townsend, Peter. *Jazz in American Culture*. Jackson: University of Mississippi Press, 2000.

Tucker, Sherrie. *Swing Shift: "All-Girl" Bands of the 1940s*. Durham, NC: Duke University Press, 2000.

Vacher, Peter. *Swingin' on Central Avenue: African American Jazz in Los Angeles*. Lanham, MD: Rowman & Littlefield, 2015.

Ward, Geoffrey C. and Burns, Ken. *Jazz: A History of America's Music*. New York: Alfred A. Knopf, 2000.

Washington State Arts Commission, "Governor's Heritage Award – Palmer Johnson ," https://www.arts.wa.gov/wp-content/uploads/2022/06/Archive-of-Honorees.pdf.

Watson, Sonny, "The Jitterbug," www.streetswing.com, Sonny Watson's Streetswing.com.

Wiedoeft, Herb. Unattributed biographical information from www.parabrisas.com/d_wiedoefth.php. Discography in www.redhotjazz.com/wiedoefto.html.

Wiedoeft, Rudy. Unattributed biographical information from www.search.com/reference/Rudy_Wiedoeft.

Willard, Patricia, "Ella Fitzgerald, Sarah Vaughan, and Billie Holiday," in *The Oxford Companion to Jazz*. Edited by Bill Kirchner. New York: Oxford University Press, 2000.

Wilson, Lyle, Kenai. *Sunday Afternoons at Garfield Park: Seattle's Black Baseball Teams, 1911–1951*. Everett, WA: Lowell Printing & Publishing, 1997.

Woodward, C. Vann. *The Strange Career of Jim Crow*. 1957. New York: Galaxy Press, 1964.

Wright, Laurie. *Mr. Jelly Lord*. Chigwell, UK: Storyville, 1980.

Wyman, Bill with Richard Havers. *Bill Wyman's Blues Odyssey: A Journey to Music's Heart and Soul*. New York: DK Publishing, 2001.

Yanow, Scott. *Duke Ellington*. New York: Friedman/Fairfax Publishers, 1999.

Yoshida, George. *Reminiscing in Swingtime: Japanese Americans in American Popular Music, 1925-1960*. San Francisco: National Japanese Historical Society, 1997.

Young, Marl. "The Amalgamation of Locals 47 and 767," *Overture,* December 1988.

Index

11 Black Aces, 38, 44, 45, 60
411 Club, 58, *59*, 75
908 Club, 70, *71*, 75

Adams, Banjoski, 82, 84
Adams, Charles, xviii, 10, 16, 20, *21*, 24, 72
Adams, Frank "Doc," 90
Adams, Jimmy, 24, *25*, 56; 60
Adams, Wayne, 20, 24, 56, *57*
Alabamians (band), 54
Alaska-Yukon-Pacific Exposition, 8, *9*
Alhambra Theater (Harlem): Melody Jones at, 92
Alhambra, Theater (Seattle), 32
Alhambra, club, 38
Allen, Henry, 10, *57*
Al's Lucky Hour Tavern, 64, 75
Amalgamation, 42, 64, 72, 96, 98, 166; final merger of Local 76 and 493, 156; Local mergers in Los Angeles, 154; new members after, 175-7; Powell Barnett's role in, 42, 172
American Bandstand, 122
American Federation of Musicians (AFM), xi; AFM Local 76, xvii-xviii, 10, 12, 40, 74, 160 ; disciplinary action of, 16, 124; early amalgamation attempts, 18; traveling dues and, 50
AFM Local 458, xvii-xviii, 2, 12, 14, 72; founding of, 10, 172; infractions, 16; locations of, 74; Powell Barnett in, 10; women in,16
AFM Local 493, xvii-xviii, 12, 16; budget of, 42; disputes in, 20, 24; "featherbedding" in, 50, 116; locations of, 74; membership list, 175-7; as Musicians' Protective Union, 72, *146*; non-blacks in, xviii, 140, 160, 172; officers of, 146, 156, 160; as "Rainbow Coalition," xviii, 140; territory controlled by, 38, 120, 130; touring bands and, 50, 112
Ammons, Gene, 152

Anderson, Don, 60
Anderson, Ernestine, xiv, 128, *129*, 148, *149*
Anderson Ivie, 50
Anzier Theater. *See* Savoy Hall
Apollo Theater (Harlem), 108, 112
"Aqua Jazz Concerts," 164
Aragon Ballroom, 124
Arcade, The (Las Vegas), 14
Archia, Tom, 98
Arlen, Harold, 168
Armstrong, Louis "Satchmo," "Pops," *41*, 54, *117, 133*; and baseball, 68; on radio, 40; in Seattle, 38, 58, 110, 116, 130, *133*
Austin, Gilbert "Punkin," 56, *57*, 70
Austin, Mrs., 10: first female union officer, 16

Bailey, Benny, 168, *169*
Bailey, Mildred, 32
Banjomania film, 28
Barbas, Pete. 162
Barbecue Pit, 70
Bargain House, 80, *81*
Barnett, Charles "Tiny," 32, *33*
Barnett, Douglas Q., xv, 32
Barnett, Powell, Jr 5, 6, 8, 10, *11,* 16, 20, 32, 72, 76, *173*; in athletic clubs, 68, 69; badge of, 42, *43;* in coal mines 2, *4* ; founds Local 458, 2; integrates Unions,10, 172; in Local 76, 154; as "Yellow Dog Democrat," xviii
Barnett, Powell, Sr., 2, *3*
Basie, Count, 20, 82, 90, 124, 144; on baseball team, 68; in Seattle, 98, 130
Basin Street Club, 98, *99*, 136
Bates, Bernice, *91*
Bebop, xviii, 42, 96, 152, 156, 160, 166,
Beck, Dave, 136
Beiderbecke, Bix, 32
Bell, Johnny L., *91*
Benjamin, Joe, 152

201

Benson, Arthur, 124
Berg's Chalet, 64
Biltmore Hotel (Los Angeles), 34
Birdland (Seattle), 74, 166
Birmingham Industrial School Band, 90
Black and Tan Club, 38, 44, *45*, 74, *101*, 124, *125*, 148
Black and Tan Jazz Orchestra, *39*
Black Hawks Orchestra, 20, *21*
Black Satin Orchestra, 20
Blackwell, Charles, 62 106, 124
Blackwell, Robert "Bumps," 62, 98, *107*, 124; Junior Band of, 106
Blake, Eubie, 32, 50
Blount, Sonny, 90
Blue Lake Park, 64
Blue Note, The, xvii, xviii, 72, 74, 88, 172; end of, 156; exterior of, *145*, *157*; integration at, 160; interior of, 144, 152
Boas, Kenny, xv, xviii, 104, 124, 160
Bobrow, Norm, 96, 110, , 164; as integrationist, 128, *129*
Bogan, Nazareth J. Jr., *91*
Booker, Sonny, 62, *63*
Borders, Baby, 60
Bostic, Earl, 164
Bovingdon, George, 154, 156
Bowman, Will, 14
Bown, Edith, 152
Bown, Patti, 92, 94, 152, *153*; with Quincy Jones, 168, *169*
Boyd, Tootie, 84, 126, *127*
Bradford, Junie, 84
Bradford, Perry, 26, *27*
Brashear, Buddy, 62, *63*, 148
Brashear, Gerald, 62, *63*, 148
Braxton, Bob, 86, *131, 134, 135*, 140; with Jive Bombers, *87*; mixed race band of, 154
Broderick, Henry, 70
Brown, Charles, 98
Brown, Vernon, 64, *65*, 96, 120, *121, 133,* 144
Brown, Wanda, 136
Brubeck, Dave, 124, 164
"Buffalo Soldiers:" Great Plains Indian name for, 150
Buford, Pops, 152, 164
Bulosan, Carlos: novelist for *America Is In The Heart*, 46, 126
Bundle of Blues film, 28
Bundy, Evelyn, 16, 18, 24
Butler Hotel, 32, 34, 36, 44
Byars, Douglas "Slits," 44

Calloway, Cab, 122; on baseball team, 68, 110; and Cotton Club Revue, 54, *55*; in Seattle, 38, 116, *118*
Campbell, Henry, 10
Canindrome (Shanghai club), 56
Carnegie Hall: Newport Jazz Festival at, 152
Carter, Benny, 96
Carver Athletic Club, 68, *69*
Catlett, Bobby, 62, *63*
Catlett, George James "Buddy," xv, 12, 82, *83*, 144; with Blackwell Junior Band, 106; with Quincy Jones band, 168, *169*; at YMCA, 42
Cayton, Madge: writes diatribe against jazz, 18
Central Avenue (Los Angeles), 20, 58; clubs on, *98*
Charles, Ray, xiv, 66, 100, 106, 148, *149*, 152
Chase, Stanley, 168
China Castle, 58
"Chitlin Circuit," 166
Christian, Charlie, 126
Civic Auditorium: Lionel Hampton at, *139*; "Swingsational" Battle of Bands at, 106
Clark, Dick, 122
Clayton, Buck, 56
Club Alabam (Los Angeles), 20
Club Lido, *135*
Club Victor, 36
Cole, Nat "King," 50, 126, 148; baseball career of, 68
Collette, William "Buddy," 86
The Colony (club), 164
Colored Waiters, Porters and Cooks Club, Inc., 124
Coltrane, John: *Live in Seattle* recording, 162
Continental Club, 128
Cooke, Sam, 106
Cornish College of the Arts, 152
Cotton Club (Los Angeles), 52
Cotton Club (New York), 54

Cotton Club (Seattle), 54
Coy, Andrus ("Ann"), 45, *46*
Coy, Gene, 38, 44, *45*, 56, 60, 76
"Crazy Blues," 26
Cron, Roz, 112, *113*
Crosby, Bing, 32
Cruise Brothers, 28
Cruise, Terry, *133*, 144, 164
Curtis Mosby Orchestra, 28

Darensbourg, Joe, 70, 82; on cruise ships, 16, 24; on radio, 40, 108
Daughters of Tabernacle, 2
Dallavo, John, 20
Dave's Fifth Avenue, 166
Davis, Aaron, 98, *99*
Davis, Maxwell, 98
Davis, Ralph G., xv, 114, *133*, 175; with Rex Stewart and Jive Bombers *105*; at Union Club, *115*, *131*
Davis, Sammy, Jr., 98
DeFillipis, Mike, xviii, 160
Demisse, Francis, 84, 94, 100
Dillon, Ida B., 156
Dixieland Theatre, 8, *9*
Door, The, 75, 164, *165*
Dorsey Brothers, 32
Dotson, R. 156
Dude Ranch, 64
Duke Ellington and Jim Crow, 76
Dunham, Katherine, 94, *95*
Durham, Allen, 44
Durham, Clyde, 44, *45*
Durham, Eddie, 110; leads All Star Girl Orchestra, 38, 112

Eastern Star, 2
Eastside Hall. *See* Birdland (Seattle)
Ebony Café, 75, *154*. *155*; and "Jam For Breakfast," 154, *155*
Edison, Thomas, 28
"Egyptian Honeymoon," 34, *35*
Elks Club (black), 20, 66, *67*, 74, 100, 124
Ellington, Duke, xiv, 82, 90, 116, *118*; at Black and Tan, 38; in Europe, 54; in film, 28; first Seattle performance, *51*; at 411 Club, 58; and segregation, 50; stars of band, 26, 44, 90, 104
Entertainer's Club, 14, 74
Ertegun, Ahmet, 50
Ertegun, Nesuhi, 50
Eubanks, Horace, 14
Evergreen Tavern, 80
Ewing, John "Streamline," 44

Fair, Frank, 70, *71*
Ferguson, Swede, 64
Fields, Ernie, 38, 110
Fields, Lucien B., 10
Fifth Avenue Theater, 30
Finnish Hall, 75, 76, *119*
Fitzgerald, Ella, 108, *109*, 110, 140
Fort Lawton, 75, 148, *149*, 150, *151*, 152
Fort Lewis, 96, 130
Four Keys, 108, *109*
Four Sharps, 62
Francoise, Myrtle "Myrt," 92, 175
Frank Roberts Four, 62
Frat Hall, 64
Frazier, Nesbit, *71*
Free and Easy (play), 168, *169*
French and Be-Bop All Stars, 148
Fuller, Merle, 126, *127*
Funderberg, William "Fundy," xiv, xv, 156; as band leader, 90, *91*, 92; as Business Agent, 86, 88; with Jive Bombers, *87*

Garfield High School, 24, 62, 64
Garfield Park, 68
Garfield Ramblers, 18, 20, 24
Garred, Milt, 148
Gayton, Emma, 26
Gayton, Leonard, 18, 24
Gershwin, George, 32
Gill, L. Elmer, xv, 88, 130, 156, 164, 175; at Fort Lewis, *131*; with Lionel Hampton, 138; owner of Ebony Café, 154, *155*
Golden West Hotel, 26, *27*, 36; Noodles Smith and, 54
Gonzales, Anita, 14
Goode, Lillian, 16
Goodman, Benny, 68; at Palomar, 122
Granz, Norman, 154
Gray, Jerry, 164

Great Lakes Naval Facility, 86, 90
Great Lakes Navy Big Band, 86, 90
Green Mill Roadhouse, 40
Green, Milton, 96, 126, *127*, 175
Greenwell, Fred, 160
Griffith, D. W., 32
Grimes, Johnny, *91*
Groves, Buddy, 84, *85*
Groves, Sirless "Sy," 84, 94, *95*, 100

Hackett, Dee Dee, 120, *121*
Hackley, Babe, 20, 60
Hall, Josie, 70, *71*
Hallelujah! movie, 28
Hamilton, Jack, 52
Hamilton, John H. "Doc," 68, 70, 75,
Hammond, John, 168
Hampton, Gladys, 52, 138
Hampton, Lionel, 50, 98, *139*, 140; first Seattle show, 52, *53*; integrates dance, 138
Handy, John, 28
Handy, W. C., 28
Hardy, Marian, 54
Harper, Ernie, 96
Harvey, Bob, 106
Hatfield, Ernest J. "Ernie," xv, 108, *109*, *141*, 156, *158*, *159*, 176; with Ella Fitzgerald, 110; travels of, 140, *142*, *143*; union cards of, *147*
Hawkins, Coleman, 26, *27*, 110
Hawkins, Erskine, 90, 110
Heath, Percy, *155*
Henderson, Fletcher, 28, 32, 54, 110
Hendricks, Dave, 20
H. F. Alexander (ship), 20, 24
Hickey, Al, 102, *103*, *121*, *131*, *134*; with Al Pierre, 65; and Jive Bombers, 86, *87*, 104, *105*
Hilbert, Al, 136, 148, 170, *171*
Hilbert, Dorothy, 136, 148
Hines, Earl "Fatha," 40, 110
Hite, Les, 50
Hodges, Johnny 144
Holden, Oscar, 14, 70
Honeysuckle, Lem, 62
Houge, Norman E., 156
Howell, Viola, 94, 170
Hoy, Bill, 70

Hubert, Traff, 160
Hughes, Virginia, xviii, 10, 16
Hurst, Oscar, 56
Hutchinson, Doc, 14

Integration, 66; in bands, 128, *129*; at Black and Tan, 38, in clubs, *151*, 166, *167*; in International Sweethearts of Rhythm, 112; Lionel Hampton and, 138; among miners, 2; Powell Barnett and, 10, 172; in Unions, xvii, xviii, 140, 160
International Musician: racist poetry in, 18
International Sweethearts of Rhythm, 110, 112, *113*
Intolerance film, 32

Jackson, Gertrude, *71*
Jackson, Leon, xviii, 10, 16
Jackson, Milt, *155*
Jackson, Morgan, 20
Jackson, Ray, 42
Jackson Street area (Seattle), xi, 22, 36, 38, 58, 66, 72, 74, 80, *81*, 88, 128, *133*, 136
Jackson Street nightclub (unnamed), 92, *93*
Jam sessions, xvii, 58, *59*, 72, 88, 130; at Black and Tan, 44, *45*; at Blue Note, 144, 152; at Ebony Café, *155*; in Los Angeles, 154
James, Harry, 68
James, Ron, 150
Jazz Singer, The, 28
Jefferson, "Princess Zenobia," 100, *101*
"Jim Crow," 197n. 41
Jitterbug dancing, 122, *123*
Jive Bombers, 86, *87*, 104, *105*
Johnson, Bessie, 14
Johnson, Budd, 44,168, *169*
Johnson, Duke, 140, *141*
Johnson, James P., 28
Johnson, Palmer, *59*, 110, 120; band member, 70, *115*; as gifted pianist, 58; as King of the Boogie Woogie, 114; plays at benefit, 76; in Shanghai, 56
Johnson, Percy. *See* George Bovingdon.
Johnson, Tyree, 44
Jolly Roger, The, 58
Jolson, Al, 28
Jones, Coty, 16

Jones, Derniece Harris "Melody," 92, *93*, 94, 148
Jones, Gay, 76
Jones, Jo, 90
Jones, Louis, 96
Jones, Quincy Delight, xiv, 12, 98, 152, 164; in Blackwell Band, 106; in Europe, 168, *169*; with Lionel Hampton, 138; at local YMCA, 42
Jones, Reginald "Jonesy," 56, *57*
Jones, Russell, 114, *115*, 120
Jones, Thad, 144
Jungle Temple Club, 60

Kamai, Edmond, 160
Kansas City Blue Blowers, 28
Kelly, Beverly, 64, 68
Kennedy Center, 152
King, Winfield, 164, 166
Kirk, Andy, *61*; with "Clouds of Joy," 60
Knights of Labor, 2
Knights of Pythia, 2
Knights of Syncopation. *See* Black Hawks Orchestra
Knights of Tabor, 2

Lacy's Dixieland Band, 8, *9*
Lafayette Theater (Harlem), 92
Laigo, Ben, 164, *165*
Laigo, Ed, 164
Lang, Eddie 32
Larkins, Al, 96, 148, *155*
Lawrence, Bruce, 32
Lee, Dave, 136
LeProtti, Sid: leads So Different Jazz Band, 76
"Let the Good Times Roll," 170
Levi, Sol: composer of "Naughty Waltz," 32
Levy's Orpheum, 12
Lewis, Big, 148
Lewis, Charles, 36
Lewis, Emmet, 96, 156
Little Richard, 106.
Lomax, Dorothy, 66, *67*, 124
Lowe, Sammy, 90
Lunceford, James Melvin "Jimmie," 82, 98, 100, 110
Lundstrem, Igor, 56
Lundstrem, Oleg, 56

Mabane, Bob, 166
MacVootie, Julius, 148
Main Event Club, 136
Mallory, Vern, 106
Manila Tropical Troubadours, 46, *47*
Mardi Gras (club), 75, 152
Marshall, Al, 120, *121*
Marshall, Bob, 65
Marshall, John, 96
Martinez, Elsie, 160
Maryknoll, The, 164
Maryland Tavern, 58
Masons, 2
Mastin, Will, 98
Mayer, W. L., 18
Maxin Trio, 148
McAdoo, Benjamin, 72
McCurdy, Robert, 16
McEnroy Ballroom (Portland), 52
McGhee, Howard, 44
McKee, Garcia "Gossie," 148
McNeely, Jay, 98
McShann, Jay, 166
McSon Trio, 148
Men of Jazz. *See* The Savoy Boys
Mercer, Johnny, 168
Metcalf, Chuck, 162
Metropolitan Theatre, 75, 128
Meyers, Vic, *37*; in politics, 36
Miley, James "Bubber," 26, *27*
Millinder, Lucky, 110, 116, *119*
Mills, Irving, 50, 54
Missouri Sheiks film, 28
Missourians, The, 54
Miyagawa, Chizuko, 56
Miyagawa, Harumi, 56
Molina, Frank, 40, 108
Montgomery, Roy Laine, 150
Moonlight Serenaders, *49*
Moore, Alton, 44
Moore Theater, 32, 75, 110, *111*
Morris, McClure "Red Mack," 44
Morrison, George, 44
Morton, Ferdinand "Jelly Roll," 14, *15*
Mt. Baker Theater (Bellingham), 30
Mount Zion Baptist Church: Junior Choir of, 62

Murphy, Dudley, 28
Murray, S. L., 10, 16
Musicians' Protective Union. *See* AFM Local 493
Musicland, 18, *19,* 20, 156; ads in, 30, *31,* 34, 36

Nanking Café, 22, *23,* 74
Nanking Orchestra, 22
Natco's Bargain House, 80, *81*
Negro Repertory Company, 94
Nerve Lifter, The, 96
New Rex Theatre, 52
New York Revue, 100
Northern Pacific Coal Company, 2
Northwest All Star Swing Concert, 128, *129*
Northwest Enterprise, The, 76, 155; ads in, *55, 59,* 114, *115,* 116, *119*; cartoon in, *79*; feature articles in, 50, *51, 53,* 62
Northwest Improvement Company, 4

Odeon Jazz Orchestra, 22, *23*
Okeh Records, 26
Olivotto, Guglielmo, 150
Orpheum Theatre (Seattle), 20, 38
Osias, Don, 166, *167*
Osias, Frank, xv, 46, *47,* 48,
Ozark Club (Great Falls, Montana), 166, *167*

Page, Bill, 70
Palomar Theater, 75, 114, *119*
Palumbi, Dick, 162
Paramount Ballroom (Shanghai), 56
Paramount Café, 80
Paramount Theater (Seattle), *55,* 75
Paris Alhambra Theater, 168, *169*
Parker, Charles "Yardbird," 166
Parrish, Avery, 90
Patricia Café (Vancouver, BC), 14
Patty Sullivan's Club (Vancouver, BC), 14
Payne, Edythe. *See* Edythe Turnham
Payne, Stan, 156, *159*
Payne's Military Band, 6
Peabody, Eddie, 30; films of, 28; radio broadcasts and recordings, 30, *31*
Peer, Ralph, 26
Penniman, Richard, *106*
Penthouse, The, 75, 162, *163*
Perkins, Noble, 100

Pete's Poop Deck, 75, 162, *163*
Petrillo, James Caesar, 124
Picou, Alphonse, 70
Pierce, Ron, 12
Pierre, Al, 96, 110, 114, 120, *121*; in baseball, 68, *69*; itinerary of, 64; orchestra of, 62, *65,* 136; Union Club of 162
Pigford, Major, 62, *63*
Plantation, The, 20
Players Club, 128
Porter, Roy, 106
Powell Barnett's Royal Colored Giants, 68, *69*
Preer, Andy, 54
Price List and Working Rules: AFM Local 493 book, 88, *89*
"Princess De Paur & Toulae," 102; with "Tahitian Voo Doo Dancers," *103*
Puzzo, Charlie, 162

Racism: Cab Calloway and, 54; at Fort Lawton, 150; in hotels, 52; in mines, 4; on radio, 40; in Unions, 18, 32; at YMCA, 42
Radney, Clifford, 148, *149*
Raglin, Alvin "Junior," 44, *45,* 96
Rawls, Lou, 106
Read, Harry, 154
Red Hot Peppers, 14
Redman, Harold, 156, *159*
Rega Orchestra, 26
Regent Hotel (Vancouver, BC), 14
Reimer, Ruth, 94
Renton Hall, 20
Richardson, Bill, 162
Richardson, Jerome, 138, *169*
Rinaldi, Bill, 128, *129,* 135; first Caucasian in Local 493, 128; joins Local 493, xviii, 160
Rinker, Al, 32
Rinker, Mildred, 32
Rizal Social Club, 48, *49,* 74, 126, *127*
Rizal, Jose, 46, 126
Roberts, Frank, 166, *167*
Robinson, Ray C., *149*. *See also* Ray Charles.
Rocking Chair, The, 74, 148
Roosevelt, Eleanor, 86
Rose, The, 148
Rose Room, 36
Roslyn, Washington, 2, *3,* 5

Roslyn Marching Brass Bands, 6, *7*
Rowell, Bruce, 26
Roth, Franz, 60
Rowles, Jimmy, 128
Royal, Marshall, 86
Royal Colored Giants, 68, *69*
Ruffin, Dick, 70
Rupe, Art, 106
Russell, Bob, 128, *129, 131, 133,*
Russell, Charlie, 70, *71*
Russell, Luis, 40, *41*
Ruther, Wyatt, 96

St. Louis Blues film, 28, *29*
Sand Point Naval Station, 86
Sand Point Navy Band, 86
Savage, John, 34
Savoy Ballroom (Harlem), 122
Savoy Boys, The, 62, *63*
Savoy Hall, 62, 74.
Schachere, Dallas, 166, *167*
Schardt, Alvin, 156
Schultz, Bud, 164, *165*
Seattle: black population, 8, 82; clubs and halls, 74-5; Filipinos in, 46, *47*, 126, 164, *165*; growth of, 8; Hawaiians in, 140, 160; Hispanics in, xviii, 160; International District, 26, 46, 126; Japanese in, 80; radio in, 40; theatres in, 94; University, 164
"Seattle Hunch," 14
Seattle Symphony Orchestra, 32
Sebastian, Frank, 52
Segregation: in AFM Locals, xvii; in baseball, 68; in hotels, 34, 50, 52; in mines, 2; in Union, 90; at YMCA, 42
Senator's Ballroom, *61*, 75, 110
Session's Playhouse, 75, 100
Shanghai: music in, 24, 56, *57*; International District, 56; restaurants in, *23*, 24, *25*, 75
Shantytown (Bellingham), 84
Shaughnessy, Ed, 152
Shaw, Freda, 16
Shepperson, James, 2, 4
Show Box, 76
Shuffle Along, 50
Sissle, Noble, 50, 110, 116, *119*

Skugstad, Jan, 160
Smith, Al, 38; dubbed "On the Scene" photographer, 92
Smith, Bessie, 26, 28, *29*
Smith, Carl "Tatti," 44
Smith, Lillian, 16
Smith, Mamie and "Her Jazz Hounds," 26, *27*
Smith, Nixie, 70
Smith, Russell "Noodles," 26, 36, 38, 44
Smith, Willie, 86
Snack Bar, The, 164
Sotero, Marjorie Polk, 150
Soul Stirrers, The, 106
Specialty Records, 106
Squires, Melvina, 70, *71*
Stafford, Jesse, 34
Stanbrough, J. J., 10
Standifer, Floyd, xviii, 94, 148, 152, 156, *161*, 177; with Blackwell band, 98, 106; contrasts AFM Locals, 160; with Quincy Jones, 168, *169*; radio buff, 40; with Thad Jones, 144; at YMCA, 42
Stephens, Ralph, 126, *127*
Stewart, Rex, 104, *105*, 144
Still, William Grant, 32
Summerville, James "Cat Eye," *91*
Sun Ra, 90
Swayzee, Edwin, 122
Sykes, Ruth, 154
"Syncopated Classic" method book, 22

Taniguchi Masaru Beer Parlor, 80
Tate, Erskine, 56
Tatum, Art, 124
Taylor, Charlie, 106
Tenth Division Patriotic Defense Council, 10
Terry, Clark, 86, 168, *169*
Tharpe, Sister Rosetta, 110
Thomas, Creon, 20, *21*, 24
Thomas, John L., 50
Thurlow, Janet, 138
Todd, Louis, 148
Todd's (club), *77*, 130, *133*
Tokiwa Hotel, 46
Tolles, Billy, *69*, 100, 122, 144; with Men of Jazz, 62, *63*
Trianon Ballroom, 34, *35*, 36, 62, 74, 148

Trumbauer, Frankie, 32
Tucker, Earl "Snakehips," 50
Tucker, Sophie, 26
Turay, Al, 44, 58, *135*, 136, *163*; at All Star Concert, *129*; at Ebony Café, *155*; at jam session, 128
Turnham, Edythe (Payne), 10, 16, 170; as band leader, *21*, 136; leads Plantation Syncopators and Dixie Aces, 20.
Turnham, Floyd, 20, *21*,
Turnham, Floyd, Jr., 20, *21*
Turnham, Maggie, 20
Twenty Ninth Special Services Band, 96
Two Pals Club, 120

Union Club, *115*, 120, 130, *131*, 162
United Federation of Miners, 2
University of Washington, 152

Valentine, Jerry, 152
Vaughan, Sarah, 152
Vaughn, Leon, *65*, 98, *99*
Venuti, Joe, 32, 164
Vernon, Lue, 18
Vidor, King, 28
Villa, Pomping, 56, *57*
Volunteers of America Marching Band, 10, *11*

Wagner, "Dad" or "Pop," 18
"Wagner's Band" poem, 18, *19*
Waldron, Frank, *13*, 16, *23*; as teacher, 12, 20, 22
Waldron School of Saxophone and Trumpet, 22
Walker, Aaron Thibeaux "T-Bone," 98
Walker, Harry, 70
Waller, Thomas "Fats," 92, 100, 110, *111*
Walton, Frank, 154
Ward, Ulysses G. "Jabo," xv, 12, 128, 144, 177; at All Star concert, *129*; at Pete's Poop Deck, 162, *163*; recalls World War II, 78; salary, 64
Washington, Dinah, 152
Washington Social and Educational Club, 74, 84, *95*, 96, *103, 104, 105*; dancers at, 94, 100, 102; national bands at, 98
Watson, Frank, 156
Weatherford, Teddy, 56
Webb, Chick, 108

Webster, Ben, 44, 58, 144
Wells, Elizabeth Dean, 70, *71*, 72, 116
Wells, Gerald, 70, *71*, 76, 110, 114, 124, 177; in bands, *77*, 96, *115*; Local 493 office at home of, 72, 116; as Local 493 President, xvii, 128; on radio, 40, 108; travels of, 76
West, Earl, 56, *57*
Westlake Music College (Los Angeles), 166
Whaley, Earl, 24; and Cotton Pickers Orchestra, 54; in Shanghai, 56, *57*
Whang Doodle Orchestra, 12, *13*
Whatley, John "Fess," 90; leads Birmingham Industrial School Band, 90
Wheeler, Harry "Doc," 86, *105*
White, Harry Alexander "Father White," 122
White, Jimmy, 140, *141, 142*
Whiteman, Paul, *33*; as "King of Jazz," 32
Whyte, Zack, 60
Wiedoeft, Adolph, 34
Wiedoeft, Gerhardt, 34
Wiedoeft, Herb, *34, 35*; leads Cinderella Roof Orchestra, 34
Wiedoeft, Rudy, 34
Wiggins, Gerald, 96, *97*, 126
Williams, Clarence "Prince of the Blues," 98, 102, *103*; sings blues, *99*, 104
Williams, Fate, 56
Williams, Ivory "Pops," 90
Williams, Luther, *91*
Williams, Mary Lou, 60, 152
Williams, Nelson, *91*
Williamson, Evelyn, 16
Williamson, Marvie, 70, *71*
Willis, John, xv, *87*, 104, *105*, 147, 177; as Local 493 Secretary-Treasurer, 86, *146*, 154, 160
Wilson, Dick, 12, 44, 60, *61*
Wilson, Gerald, 20
Wilson, Teddy, 20
Winburn, Anna Mae, 112, *113*
Winslow, Zelma, 16
Witwer, John, 156
Women in Jazz Festival, 152
Woods, Phil, 168, *169*
Woodmen of the World (W.O.W.), 12
WPA Federal Theater Project, 94
Wright, Gertrude Harvey, 16, *17*

Wright, Robert, 38, *39*, 44
Yukon Club, 120, 136

YMCA, 42, 75
Yoshijima, Yukiko, 80
Young, Cecil, 66
Young, Lester, 68, 94